LEE GJERTSEN MALONE

# THE LAST BOY AT ST. EDITH'S

**ALADDIN**
NEW YORK   LONDON   TORONTO   SYDNEY   NEW DELHI

ALADDIN

An imprint of Simon & Schuster Children's Publishing Division

1230 Avenue of the Americas, New York, New York 10020

First Aladdin hardcover edition February 2016

Text copyright © 2016 by Lee Gjertsen Malone

Jacket illustration copyright © 2016 by Paul Hoppe

All rights reserved, including the right of reproduction in whole or in part in any form.

ALADDIN is a trademark of Simon & Schuster, Inc., and related logo is a registered trademark of Simon & Schuster, Inc.

For information about special discounts for bulk purchases, please contact Simon & Schuster Special Sales at 1-866-506-1949 or business@simonandschuster.com.

The Simon & Schuster Speakers Bureau can bring authors to your live event. For more information or to book an event contact the Simon & Schuster Speakers Bureau at 1-866-248-3049 or visit our website at www.simonspeakers.com.

Book designed by Laura Lyn DiSiena

The text of this book was set in Janson.

Manufactured in the United States of America 0116 FFG

10 9 8 7 6 5 4 3 2 1

Library of Congress Cataloging-in-Publication Data

Malone, Lee Gjertsen.

The last boy at St. Edith's / by Lee Gjertsen Malone.

p. cm.

Summary: Seventh-grader Jeremy Miner, the only boy in a school of 475 girls, unleashes a series of pranks in hopes of getting expelled.

[1. Schools—Fiction. 2. Practical jokes—Fiction. 3. Friendship—Fiction.

4. Massachusetts—Fiction.] I. Title. II. Title: Last boy at Saint Edith's.

PZ7.1.M35Las 2016

[Fic]—dc23

2015022675

ISBN 978-1-4814-4435-4 (hc)

ISBN 978-1-4814-4437-8 (eBook)

**For Scott and Nora**

# PREP CONFIDENTIAL

**RED MILL, MA:** School's just starting up again for the plaid-skirt and clip-on-tie masses here in western Massachusetts, and if it's anything like last year, we're looking forward to another round of juicy gossip and sometimes even actual news. But the big question on our mind is, what's going on at St. Edith's Academy? We know—nobody cares about the state of that dismal place except for the humor value of its miserable attempt at going coed. But ever since last year, after its roster of boys dwindled to fewer than have actually set foot on the moon, we here at the *Con* knew that the writing was on the proverbial wall. And now, rumor has it, only two unfortunate males have managed to enroll for the coming semester. Which begs the question: Who will be next?

Or, more accurately, who will be *last*?

# ONE

**IT WAS THE THIRD DAY OF THE NINTH WEEK OF** school when Jeremy Miner decided to get kicked out of seventh grade.

He'd been sitting on a school bus waiting to go to MacArthur Prep to cheer on his sister Rachel and the rest of the St. Edith's championship volleyball team. He'd been late, one of the last people on the bus, which meant he had to sit up front behind Mr. Reynolds.

Jeremy probably should have liked Mr. Reynolds more than he did. Reynolds was the language arts teacher, and Jeremy loved to read, not to mention he was the only male teacher at the school and the faculty advisor of the Film Club, Jeremy's favorite after-school activity.

But there was something irritating about Reynolds. Maybe it was the fussy way he laid his finger next to his mouth when he was listening to a student, or how he called Jeremy "Mr. Miner" with such overpronounced emphasis on the "Mr." that the girls in the back of the class would titter.

The driver was starting to close the door when Claudia darted onto the bus and slid into the seat next to Jeremy, the yard of ball chain wrapped around her neck and wrists looking like armor in contrast to the shredded pink tights she wore under her plaid skirt.

"Did you hear?" she hissed.

Claudia Hoffmann was one of Jeremy's best friends. She was a year older than everyone else in their grade because her mother was Italian and her father was German and they'd lived in London, New Zealand, and Hong Kong when she was little. Somewhere along the way she missed a year of school. Claudia sometimes took the extra year as permission to dominate everyone else. (Not that she actually needed permission to do what she wanted most of the time.)

"No, what?"

"Andrew Marks transferred to Hereford Country Day."

Jeremy let out a long breath and slumped down in his seat. "Oh no."

Jeremy hadn't particularly liked Andrew—nobody did—he brushed his teeth only about once a week, for one, and he talked about the Boston Red Sox far more than any one person should ever talk about anything. Andrew was the kind of guy Jeremy's mom always said he should "make an effort with" and "try to get to know better." But Jeremy figured that probably meant spending more time with Andrew, and since the time they spent together as the sole members of the boys' tennis team was already pretty tedious, he couldn't see how hanging out even more would improve things.

But Andrew did have one redeeming quality—he was male.

Because Jeremy had a girl problem. Or, more accurately, a *girls* problem. Four hundred and seventy-five of them, including his older sister, Rachel, who was in the eighth grade, and his younger sister, Jane, who was in fourth. That's how many girls went to St. Edith's Academy.

At home it was just his mom and his sisters. Jeremy's dad was off saving the oceans in his solar-powered research boat. And now the only other boy in school had thrown in the towel, a day Jeremy had dreaded for two whole years.

"Why'd he transfer now?" Jeremy demanded, loud enough that Reynolds's head poked up over the seat. He lowered his voice. "Why not over the summer?"

"I guess he was on a waiting list?" Claudia said. "Or maybe he came back and everybody else was gone and he decided to bail. Who knows? Andrew Marks is a moron."

"You only say that because he never wanted to be in your movies."

"No," she said, cocking her head. "I say that because it's undeniably true. He likes bad rap and professional wrestling. But that's not the issue."

"You bet that's not the issue. Besides, lots of boys like stuff like that—"

"You don't," she said.

He ignored the interruption. He was used to them with Claudia. "The point is now I'm the last boy in the whole entire school."

Jeremy had a list, buried deep in his desk drawer at home. Twenty-six names. A list of all the boys who had attended St. Edith's. He'd made it in fifth grade, when they'd all pledged to transfer or get kicked out.

He'd vowed not to be the last one. Over the years he'd added a number to each of their names as they left, counting down, one by one, from twenty-six, every time swearing he would be next. But now his list was down to number two, Andrew Marks. And there was only one name left: Jeremy's.

It was never supposed to come to this. He'd always hoped that his mom would let him transfer, or that some of the other boys would hang on until the end of eighth grade. Being one of a few boys, even if he didn't especially like any of them, was manageable. Being the only boy was something else entirely.

St. Edith's was what you might call a failed experiment. Founded in 1879 as an all-girls school—the words ACADEMY FOR GIRLS were still carved in the limestone above the imposing front doors—but faced with declining admissions, the board of trustees had decided to start admitting boys right before Jeremy was old enough for first grade.

But few boys ever wanted to attend. The school had a long-standing reputation as a staid and chaste academy for girls that no amount of rebranding could change. And the failure to attract male students meant boys' sports suffered, which made it even harder to convince boys to come.

In a last-ditch effort, the trustees added a football team as a way to attract boys who wanted to play but perhaps would not have made the team at other, more sports-savvy schools. The problem was a football team needed thirty or forty kids to be really viable, and there were only fifty-two boys in the whole school, with only about twenty old enough to play.

So, in a controversial move that was infamous in the annals of western Massachusetts private schools, the trustees decided to make football mandatory.

Mandatory football was a disaster right from the start.

They didn't call it that, of course. They called it "Fulfilling the physical education requirement through team sport," and they made all the girls play on teams too, to make it fair. But it basically meant mandatory football for all the boys in seventh and eighth grade.

The football coach was Ms. Brewster, who also coached the badminton and lacrosse teams and seemed to think the only differences in football were the shape of the ball and a little bit of tackling. This was a catastrophic error, as seen in the team's first game against coed MacArthur Prep.

Tiny seventy-five-pound seventh graders were crushed by onrushing linebackers. A boy who had never run for anything, not even a bus, collapsed, wheezing, in the end zone. And James McPhee, whose family had emigrated from Ireland and who was under the impression he was learning to play a slightly more physical version of soccer, saw the line of broad-shouldered players from the other team steaming down the field toward him, turned, and ran off, never to be heard from again.

Their team name—the Amazons—didn't help either.

Jeremy was only in fourth grade at the time, so he wasn't forced to play. Instead he stood dumbly on the sidelines, holding his embarrassing French horn, and prayed they would cancel mandatory football before he was old enough to join the team.

He got his wish.

Boys complained and convinced their parents to transfer them to one of the many other successful coed or all-boys schools in the area, and a few short years after it first added boys, right before Jeremy started fifth grade, St. Edith's gave up and went back to being all-girls. The school would allow the existing boys who attended to continue on and graduate but would admit no more.

*Prep Confidential*—the private-school insider blog all students read religiously—had a field day.

The *Con*, as it was called, was never a fan of St. Edith's, which it called St. Dither's Nunnery and reviewed as a school for "girls whose parents want to give them an education in the most charmless and fun-free setting possible," noting "what passes for excitement at St. Dither's would count as detention at other schools."

After the attempt to turn coed, the blog became even more vicious, writing "for the misguided few boys who wanted to attend this dour institution, the single season of mandatory football killed that desire, along with, for many, the will to live."

The parents and teachers—including the newly installed post-football-debacle director, Ms. Powell—said not to take what the *Con* wrote so seriously.

"Everybody knows the people who write those reviews aren't basing their findings on actual facts," Jeremy's mother said. "And who cares what a website says, anyway? The teachers are just as good at St. Edith's as anywhere else, and that's the only thing that's important."

Of course, it wasn't the only thing that was important, not by a long shot, and every time the *Con* wrote about St. Edith's, enrollment fell and more students transferred. Especially boys.

In fact, right after the decision to go back to all-girls status there had been a mass exodus of almost every remaining male, except for a hardy few who, by fate or circumstance, were forced to remain: Jeremy's list of twenty-six.

It had been pointless to hope that these same souls would hang on until graduation. The truth had been dawning since the first day of school when Jeremy discovered that over the summer even Carson Johnson and Elijah Rosen (number three and number four, respectively) had both transferred, leaving just Jeremy and smelly Andrew Marks.

And now just Jeremy.

He glanced around the bus, where, as usual, he and the teacher were the only people with a Y chromosome. "I'm going to spend the rest of my life surrounded by girls."

"You say that like it's a bad thing," Claudia said with a fake glare. "Why do you even want to go to school with boys? You weren't friends with most of the boys who went here, anyway."

She had a point. Even back when there were a couple dozen boys in the school, he had mainly hung out with

Claudia and her crowd. Really, he hadn't had a guy friend since fifth grade, when Miles Portman (number twenty) moved to Minnesota. But somehow it was different when they were younger. Hanging out with only girls wasn't a problem when they were still little kids.

It was only lately he'd really begun to notice.

"It's not just about friends," he said. "Though I think if I had half the school to choose from I might actually meet some guys I liked. It's more about not wanting to stand out so much. Having a . . . buffer zone."

"A buffer zone?" Claudia asked with a quizzical look.

"Something to stand between me and being a total freak of nature." He paused, then pressed on. "But it's not just that. What about getting to do things boys do? Having a boys' bathroom instead of being forced to use the one in the office. And what about the tennis team? It's the only sport I actually like. How can we have a team with only one player? Barely anybody wanted to play against us when it was just Andrew and me."

There were so many reasons he felt out of place at St. Edith's. Always having to draw girls in art, because those were the only models—and the girls making faces at his drawings, either in mockery or disgust. Not to mention talking about the endless list of topics the girls insisted on in health class while he put his fingers in his ears and hummed. Or being forced to play field hockey in gym. "Men play field hockey all over the world!" Miss Carter, the gym teacher, liked to say whenever she brought out the equipment. "Australia, India, England—everywhere."

"But not here," Jeremy always grumbled. It was a constant reminder he didn't belong at St. Edith's, learning a sport most people played in skirts. What people like Claudia didn't understand was that all he really wanted was to be a regular guy, someone who fit in.

She gave him a sympathetic shrug, but even she didn't have an answer.

A few moments later the bus turned down the long drive leading to the impressive facade of MacArthur Prep, the fiercest rival of St. Edith's. Well, in girls' sports. Because unlike Jeremy's school, MacArthur was coed. And events at coed schools were always the worst.

But he had to go to the game; his sister was the star of the team. The financial aid director at St. Edith's had already confided in Jeremy's mom that she expected "lots of interest" from high schools who wanted a student like Rachel, with top-notch grades and the potential to be all-American in volleyball and field hockey. And lots of interest meant lots of scholarships, which was the only way Rachel would get to go to any of those places, Jeremy knew.

As they made their way into the gym and onto the bleachers, he stayed deep within a gang of St. Edith's girls. Once Reynolds and the other teachers were distracted, he slipped off his telltale baby-blue-and-pale-yellow plaid school tie and stuffed it into his pocket. Not that he'd be getting up at all during the game—he knew better than to leave his seat.

The last time he got up at one of Rachel's volleyball games, last year, he and David Somers (number eleven) had been cornered by a couple of kids in the bathroom who told them they should be using the girls' room instead and, for good measure, escorted David down the hall and stuck his face in one of the girls' toilets. He transferred out two days later.

This time Jeremy went in with a plan: Lie low, stay in the middle of the pack, and attract as little attention as possible.

And it seemed to work. At least until the third set.

"You love those Batman movies, but you know what drives me crazy?" Claudia was saying. She wasn't even pretending to watch the match. "Bruce Wayne is a really famous rich guy! Everybody knows who he is. So how can he just fake his death, skip town, and go hang out in a café in Paris? It would be like Elvis showing up for the breakfast special at Denny's in Daytona Beach. Don't you think at least someone would notice? Don't they have paparazzi in Gotham City?"

"Hey, look," a boy's voice called from a few rows away. "Is it just me, or are the St. Edith's girls getting uglier? That one looks like a dude." It was one of the MacArthur Prep boys, and his voice was loud enough that everyone in their section looked over. Too loud, really, to be anything but trouble.

"Ha-ha, you're hilarious," Claudia said in the direction of the voice.

The speaker was sitting with a whole gang of boys, all wearing the same sharp-looking navy blazers and gray pants that marked them as going to MacArthur and made Jeremy glad he'd taken off his ugly pastel tie.

He poked Claudia with his elbow to get her to shut up and pretended to be completely captivated by the action on the volleyball court.

But he heard rustling and grumbling down the row as the loud boy shoved his way past the plaid-covered St. Edith's knees and squeezed in right between Jeremy and Claudia. He threw a large arm around Jeremy's shoulders, like they were friends, but the weight of it sent a current of panic down Jeremy's spine.

"So, tell me, what's it like being a boy at a girls' school?" the boy said in a low voice, too close to Jeremy's face. His breath was a gag-inducing combination of old milk and Doritos. "Are you turning into one yet?"

Jeremy laughed like the kid was joking, even though he clearly wasn't. Around him the girls tittered into their hands and moved away, all except Claudia, who was widening her eyes at Jeremy like she was trying to communicate with him telepathically.

"Do you think I'm funny?" the guy said, suddenly way more affronted than he could possibly really be. "Do you want to start something with me? Do you have something to prove, lady boy? Because if you want to start something, let's do it. Come on outside, and we'll see how funny I am."

Jeremy squirmed. "No, I just . . ."

The guy leaned back and spread his knees wide, taking up enough bleacher for two people. "A guy like you, surrounded by all these chicks," he said with a smirk. "What a waste. If it was me, I'd have them eating out of my hand."

There was some grumbling from the girls and another pointed look from Claudia. Jeremy felt ill. Attracting attention at a place like this was the last thing he wanted.

The boy snorted. "I bet you don't even have a girlfriend."

Jeremy winced. It's not like he actually wanted a girlfriend; he had enough problems dealing with girls just as friends and classmates. But it wasn't the sort of thing you wanted someone to say out loud in front of half the school.

"I bet you're too busy painting your toenails and watching, like, *Frozen* with your lady friends," the boy continued with an ugly little smile at Claudia, who looked like she was holding her breath to keep from exploding. Jeremy wasn't sure if it was because she was aching to defend her friend against this bully or because he had accused her of liking a Disney film.

And now the boy was looking at him like he expected

Jeremy to say something back. Jeremy gulped. He had no idea how to respond to a guy like this. It was cold in the gym, but sweat formed on the back of Jeremy's neck as the boy kept smiling at him in a really unfriendly way. Jeremy could think of a million wrong things to say but nothing that could possibly make this boy leave him alone.

And the seconds ticked by.

Then one of the other boys called from down the row, "Mike, let's go, I want a soda."

The boy named Mike smiled at Jeremy and stood. "Looks like it's your lucky day. I've got to go. Besides, my dad always told me I shouldn't hit a girl."

Claudia made a face at his retreating back. "Guys like that make me eternally grateful I go to an all-girls school."

"Hey!" Jeremy said, even though he was still trying to force his breathing back to normal. He knew the boy wouldn't have done anything really bad with all the teachers around, but he was still rattled. It was always like this with boys who went to normal schools.

"I kid, I kid. But at least I got an actual reaction from you." She gave him a piercing look. "Seriously, why didn't you say something? Instead of just . . . sitting there."

"Great, why don't you try and make me feel even more horrible?" he said. "Especially since it's just going to get worse now that Andrew's gone. I'm lucky I'm not spending the rest of the match with my head in a toilet."

The next two years spread out ahead of him, a series of unrelenting humiliations. No more boys' teams to play on. The only boy in yellow and baby blue at sporting events. The only boy on their side of the gym at those ridiculous dances his friends claimed were lame but always wanted to attend. The only boy at graduation, the only boy at every party and in every class play.

The only boy, anywhere and everywhere, standing out like a sore thumb. For what felt like the rest of his life.

And the worst part was, lately he was beginning to wonder what it meant to be, if not a man, then a guy who was going to be one someday. How did you even figure that out when you were surrounded by girls all the time? From movies? Even an orphan like Luke Skywalker had Uncle Owen to look up to. As for real life, he wasn't clueless enough to aspire to be like the guys at MacArthur Prep, but it wasn't like he had any other alternatives—even if he wanted to be a sensitive guy, how would he learn? His sensitive dad had skipped out years ago without leaving anything like a guidebook behind.

"Okay. I get it. Your life stinks. So what do you plan to do about it?" Claudia asked.

"That's the problem," Jeremy said, shaking his head. "I don't know."

# TWO

**THE WIND BLEW ORANGE AND RED LEAVES OFF**
the trees as Jeremy biked furiously home after the game.
The colors were ridiculously bright against a wide blue sky
dotted with clouds. He could see the beauty but felt separate from it all.

Rachel was having pizza with the rest of the volleyball
team, and Jane was still at school waiting for their mother,
who was a secretary there. She was supposed to be taking
the minutes for a meeting of a new committee Director
Powell had formed. It was called the Legacy Committee,
though Jeremy's mom mainly called it the Idiot Committee.

So today he was on his own, biking the two miles from
the hilly campus of St. Edith's to his house in the next town
over. He didn't mind the ride. He needed time to think.

First he rode through the village, with its brick store-
fronts and wrought-iron benches. Red Mill, where St. Edith's
was located, called itself "the prettiest village in western
Massachusetts" and even had signs all over town proclaim-
ing so, something that caused frustration and the occasional

rumbling about lawsuits from other, equally attractive towns whose leaders believed the nickname should have been at least voted on or something.

Nobody would call Lower Falls, where Jeremy lived, the prettiest town in anywhere. If Red Mill was the sort of place Bostonians who'd made a killing in finance moved to to open art galleries and send their kids to prep schools, then Lower Falls was where they went to get a crack in their windshield fixed at one of the body shops out by the old railroad tracks.

That's why even with Andrew Marks gone, Jeremy knew his mother would never let him transfer. She was a school secretary, which was how he and his sisters managed to go to St. Edith's in the first place—they got free tuition, part of a staff scholarship program nobody else but his family ever applied for. Without that scholarship, they would have had to go to the local public school, what his mother called "that" school: Warren G. Harding Junior/Senior High.

The school had been in the news recently thanks to a spate of violent fistfights among a gang of girls. News stories abounded, all using words and phrases like "gritty" and "former mill town" and "depressed area of the Berkshires."

The kids at St. Edith's spread even worse rumors about Harding. About kids stuffed into lockers—which Jeremy couldn't picture, because the lockers at St. Edith's were only about a foot square—and someone getting robbed right in the middle of the cafeteria by a classmate wielding a sharpened butter knife, plus one often-repeated story about a teacher who flipped out so badly over his class's behavior that he had to be escorted out of the school in a straitjacket.

"There is no possible way you are ever going to that school, even if I got hit by a truck," Jeremy's mother had announced a few weeks earlier, clicking off the TV news program featuring the fights at Harding. "Look at those girls! Are they the kind of kids you want to surround yourself with? At a school like that?"

Jeremy had seen pictures of the girls who got into fights at Harding, and he thought he could say with complete certainty none of them would ever hang out with him whether he went to school there or not. Beat him up, maybe.

But that didn't matter to his mother. It only furthered her resolve to keep him at St. Edith's until graduation, when hopefully his good grades would earn him a scholarship to a private high school.

Which is why he needed to take more drastic measures.

Jeremy biked past Red Mill's tea shops and dog boutiques, then cut around its small cemetery with dark and ancient headstones littered with orange leaves, like a Halloween display in a variety store, until he reached a long stretch where the bike lane ended. Now he was riding on the shoulder next to nothing but trees and brush. This was his favorite part, where he could be alone except for the occasional car veering into the opposite lane to avoid him.

Then the road opened up again, and there were car dealerships and overgrown train tracks and in the distance tall, thin, brick smokestacks that hadn't smoked in years, the buildings themselves turned into condos and old folks' homes. Lower Falls.

When he reached his house, he went straight to his room, in the back, across from his mother's. The girls shared the upstairs, an attic space with a sloping roof. That plus a living room and an eat-in kitchen was pretty much the whole place.

He threw his backpack on his bed, rummaged through his desk drawers, and pulled out his list of the remaining boys at St. Edith's. He took a pen, crossed out Andrew Marks, and wrote number two next to his name. He hadn't liked a lot of these guys, it was true. But he'd been unhappy to see every single one of them go. Number twenty-six, Will James, once invited all the boys in their class on a big camping trip, before his parents sent him to boarding school. Number twenty-one, Carlos Martins-Diaz, tried to get the school to start a Boy Scouts troop, but not enough people were interested. Jeremy wasn't sure where he'd gone, but he imagined a place filled with boys whittling wood and helping little old ladies cross the street. Number fourteen, Matt Kepler, had been the only boy shorter than Jeremy in sixth grade. He went to MacArthur Prep now and pretended he didn't know Jeremy when they ran into each other at Rachel's volleyball games.

Each of them had faced the same humiliations Jeremy did, day in and day out, and each of them had cracked under the pressure. And now Jeremy was the only one left.

He ripped up the list. He didn't need it anymore and looking at it made his head hurt.

Instead he grabbed his notebook and wrote a title across the top of a fresh piece of paper, like he was writing an essay for school. He almost put his name underneath but stopped himself. This was a secret document. The thought made him smile, but the smile faded as he contemplated the pros and cons.

HOW TO GET KICKED OUT OF SCHOOL

1. Set a Fire

Pros: Immediate. Dramatic.

Cons: How do you set fire to an almost 150-year-old stone building?

Jeremy had no idea. It wasn't like he set things on fire recreationally all that often. Or ever, actually. Also, he might end up going to juvenile hall instead of getting to transfer to public school.

And what if someone got hurt? Or his mom lost her job? And if he burned down the school, then his sisters wouldn't be able to go there either. And maybe Jane would end up being one of those tough townie girls, with drawn-on eyebrows and hair scraped back into painfully tight ponytails, who stood around smoking on the corner near the donut shop, and Jeremy's mother would blame him forever.

2. Start a Fight with Someone
Pros: ???

Jeremy had trouble thinking of any. He hated fights. All the rocking back and forth and shoving. But maybe people would think he was tough if he got in a fight? It could improve his reputation. And he might have to learn how to fight at least a little bit if he went to a coed school.

Cons: The juvie thing again.

Plus he was the only boy in the building. And while there were a few girls he'd like to see get punched in the face, he had to be realistic—the only ones it would be fair to start something with would probably win.

3. Flunk Out
Pros: This would hurt no one but me, and

I wouldn't have to punch anybody.

Cons: Time-consuming.

Jeremy got practically all As. It would take months, maybe even the whole year, to fail. Also, if he flunked, then he'd never get a scholarship to high school, and was getting out of St. Edith's worth that?

If only his mother could figure out a way to send him somewhere else—anywhere. But his mom was, well, his mom. Frazzled. Next to impossible to talk to. Always saying "I don't want to yell" and then turning around and yelling like five seconds later.

He stared at the paper for a minute, then ripped it out of his notebook and crunched it into a ball. He almost tossed it in the trash can but instead dropped it back on his desk.

Voices were coming down the hall. His mother was home. He should probably go talk to her—again—about how he felt, before he did anything drastic. But it seemed so pointless.

"The girls . . . they're just too . . . distracting," he'd said once, trying a different tack.

"Distracting how? Do they talk in class? Because I know you talk in class. I've had more than one teacher mention it. So don't think for a second you can blame the girls for that."

"No," he said patiently. Or somewhat patiently. Patience was hard with his mother. "Well, yes, they do, but that's not it. It's more because they're girls that's distracting. To me."

But she just laughed at him. It wasn't a mean laugh—his mother was a lot of things, but she wasn't mean, exactly—but it was still a laugh, that knowing and loud laugh grown-ups do when they think kids are being funny even though to the kid the situation is not funny *AT ALL*.

"Honestly, Mom, you have to admit it's a little weird," Rachel had chimed in. "How would you feel if you were the only woman in a place full of men?"

"That actually happens more than you think, Rachel," she said, her tone serious again. "Besides, it's not that I'm not sympathetic. I know it's not the ideal situation. But, Jeremy, you're going to live in a world surrounded by women your whole life! You'll have to study with girls in college and work with women when you grow up. Maybe, if you're lucky, you'll find someone who wants to spend the rest of their life with you, and that person might be a woman too. At some point you're going to need to learn how to deal with them as people. Fifty percent of the population is female!"

"Fifty percent," he had argued. "Not one hundred percent."

It was no use. He couldn't really explain—not to his mother. In fact, he strongly suspected she thought this total-girl immersion experience was good for him, like she was making sure he wouldn't be a macho jerk when he grew up—her own little feminist science project.

He wandered to the kitchen and paced listlessly as his mother set down her purse, took off her coat, and stuck a carton of milk in the fridge.

"You seem quiet," she said. "How was school?"

"Andrew Marks transferred," he said, not looking at her.

"Your tennis friend? Sorry to hear that," she said, pulling a pan out of the cupboard.

"He wasn't my friend," Jeremy said with an eye roll she didn't catch. "But that's not important. Because now I'm the last boy."

"Really?" his mother asked. "I thought there were more." Her tone was light, like they were talking about the weather. Infuriating.

Jeremy shut his eyes. "You really have no idea, do you?"

She turned to look at him. "Well, why don't you try me? Give me some idea."

He let out a long breath. "Okay, how about the fact that every single day the volleyball team laughs at me. Every single day." They were eighth graders, like Rachel, and they always seemed to be headed into the first floor bathroom in a pack whenever he walked by. He knew they were laughing at him; he could hear the echoes off the tile walls, and the sound followed him all the way down the hall.

"They're not laughing at you! They probably don't even notice you." His mother opened the fridge and stared at its contents without taking anything out.

"Oh, they're laughing at me," he said grimly. He didn't know how he knew, but he knew.

Rachel walked in, hair wet from showering and looking as well put together in pink sweats as she did in her school uniform. Jane trailed behind her. "Who laughs at you?"

Jeremy's mother rolled her eyes. "The volleyball team, apparently. They are persecuting your brother by laughing in his vicinity."

"I need you to sign this form for my field trip," Jane said, ignoring the conversation entirely.

"Can't you see I'm right in the middle of making dinner?" their mother said. Jane looked around, probably confused since there was no actual evidence of food preparation anywhere in the kitchen. "Fine, just let me find a pen."

Jeremy's mother went over to a drawer and started rummaging. "Rachel, these girls are your friends. Why don't you talk to them? Tell them they're making Jeremy self-conscious—"

"Oh God no," Jeremy and Rachel said at the same time with such force their mother laughed.

"Okay, okay, bad idea," she said. "But maybe I could make some calls? Like to Allie's mom? She seems nice."

Jeremy groaned.

"Well, fine then. If you won't let me help, I don't know what you expect."

"You could let me go to another school?" he offered. "I

mean, now I'm the *only* boy at St. Edith's. That has to be a good reason to transfer."

At this, the bemused expression his mother had worn through most of the conversation immediately vanished.

"You know I can't, Jeremy," she started, and it sounded like she was going to get mad. But she just sighed, and her voice changed. "I'm doing the best I can, okay? Give me some credit, please."

"It wouldn't have to be the public school"—he knew all too well how his mother felt about Harding—"but maybe someplace like MacArthur Prep? I could get a scholarship."

She sighed in that deep, heavy way he hated. "Do you think scholarships to MacArthur grow on trees? There's a waiting list for the waiting list. And even with financial aid, there are all sorts of fees at a place like that, and we'd have to figure out how to get you there and back every day, plus you'd need completely new uniforms. I can barely keep up with the three of you at St. Edith's, and I get almost everything covered because I'm staff. There's no way we could afford it. I'm sorry."

"How do you know? I mean, we've never even tried—"

It was the wrong thing to say.

"Try? Try? You want me to try?" She laughed, but not her full and happy laugh. This time it sounded hard, like a bark. "All I do is try. I'm sorry it's not good enough for you."

Rachel jumped in. "That's not what he meant to say, Mom." She shot Jeremy a look that told him to keep his mouth shut. "He's just asking; he doesn't understand."

His sister's calming tone seemed to help. When Jeremy's mother turned to look at him, her voice was softer and firmer. "Look, Jeremy, I know it's not what you want. You've made that abundantly clear, time and time again. But it's the best we can do right now. You get an excellent private school education for free. If you want, we can start going back to the YMCA or something so you could play basketball? Meet some other boys that way?"

Jeremy had no interest in joining the Y, but he nodded listlessly. "Sure, Mom, that would be great."

She slammed shut the drawer she'd been searching. "Why can't I find anything around this place?" she asked, and went into the living room.

"She does kind of have a point, as surprising as that is," Rachel said.

"I heard that," their mother called.

"What I mean is, you complain and complain, but you never want to actually do anything to fix your problems. It's like you want to be stuck."

He shook his head. What could Rachel know? Perfect Rachel was never stuck. Even though she faced the same pressures he did to earn good grades and get into a good high school, she didn't really understand. And they'd been a team for years, ever since she stopped calling him Germy and they both realized it would take more than just their stressed-out mother to hold the family together. Rachel tried, of course. She was more sympathetic than almost anyone. But there's no way she could truly get it.

"I just asked Mom to let me switch schools. How is that not doing anything?"

"You wander in here and ask her to let you go to MacArthur just as she's walking in from work, the absolute worst time to ask Mom for literally anything," Rachel said. "You call that trying?"

He shrugged.

"I get it; I do," she said. "I mean, I wouldn't want to be you either. But if Mom won't let you transfer, I don't know what else we can do. If it makes you feel better, I don't think most of the girls at school even notice you're there." She caught the look on his face and added, "No offense."

As though that wasn't half the problem. Even when there had been other boys, everything at St. Edith's was completely geared toward girls—what they thought, what they needed, what they wanted. The books they read in English class, the topics they learned about in health. For Jeremy, it was like being on display and invisible at the exact same time.

It's not like he wanted to be a superstar like Rachel or Claudia. Or the captain of a sports team or top of his class. He just wanted to be normal, whether it was at MacArthur Prep or some other school or even Harding. Was that really so wrong?

Jeremy opened the back door and walked out into the yard. There were a couple of Adirondack chairs out there, weathered and broken. When his dad had still been around they used to take them inside after summer ended and store them in the basement, but somewhere along the way that stopped, and now they were beaten soft and creaky by years of snow.

He stared at the trees in the fading sun and at the rusted

metal swing set and his little sister's old plastic ride-on toy, long abandoned, and wondered what his dad would do if he were around. How things would have been different if his father had never taken off on his boat.

It had been so long since he'd seen him that Jeremy had trouble picturing his face. Even when he'd been living at home, his father always had one foot out the door.

Mr. Miner was, at least in theory, a grad student. A "perpetual grad student" Jeremy's mother liked to say, because he'd never finished his thesis. She always said it like she also meant he was still a child—that he had never grown up.

His specialty was marine biology. "Who studies marine biology one hundred miles from the sea?" his mother would say, making that face she only ever made when she talked about Jeremy's father. "But I guess I thought it was romantic. I should have known he'd take off on a boat, eventually."

One time when his parents were fighting, he heard his father accuse his mother of not believing in him anymore. At the time, Jeremy had thought it meant like not believing in Santa, and he was mystified.

But now that he was older, Jeremy realized he hadn't been all that far off the mark. One day his mother had stopped believing like you stop believing in Santa Claus or the tooth fairy, and like those things, his father had disappeared. It was almost as if he had never been there at all.

But thinking about his dad wasn't going to help him solve his current dilemma. What he needed was a plan.

Who could help him? Emily? She was one of his best friends, even if they didn't really hang out as much as they used to. She lived in the house behind his, and she'd always been there, like the trees in his backyard and the mountains in the distance.

But Emily was a law-abiding girl, serious and studious and not at all a person who would approve of him getting expelled. Claudia said she was a dork and it was kind of true, and not in a cool way either. But he could see the back of Emily's house through the dusk, and the light was on in her room. He had to at least try.

"I'm going to Emily's," he yelled at the back door, but didn't stop to listen to the muffled reply.

# THREE

**JEREMY CUT THROUGH THE STRAGGLY BITS OF** brush at the rear of their property and around the neat fence surrounding Emily's and let himself into the yard. He walked into the kitchen without knocking, as usual, and, with a wave at Emily's mother, hidden behind her laptop, went upstairs to Emily's room. Emily's house was larger than his, with a couple of bedrooms on the second floor and a real dining room and a den for watching movies downstairs, even though it was just for Emily and her parents.

Her house was always a little too warm. There was a bowl of hard candy on the coffee table no one ever ate, and the sofa's slipcovers shifted awkwardly when you moved. But the two of them would sit there for hours with an afghan on their knees, sharing a bowl of microwave popcorn and watching TV after their homework was done. It was a ritual they'd engaged in since kindergarten, since before Jeremy ever thought of Emily as a girl.

When they were younger, he and Emily used to play

with her dog, Princess Di, trying to figure out if there was anything a dog wouldn't eat. They didn't feed her anything poisonous or that she could choke on, just unusual things. This was how they learned that Princess Di liked dill pickles, peanut brittle, cherry Jell-O, raspberry limeade, and figs stuffed with cream cheese. On the no list were jalapeño peppers, sliced lemons, and saltwater taffy. They hadn't played that game in over a year, but Princess Di still greeted him eagerly at the top of the stairs, waiting for treats.

Most people who saw Emily's room would probably agree with Claudia's assessment of her dorkiness. The walls were covered with posters of TV shows for little kids, and she had way too many stuffed animals for someone who was twelve. Especially since they all had names.

But she was also into interesting anime movies and collected tiny toys from Japan. Those were the sorts of things Claudia and Delaney and Tabitha would have thought were cool if it was anybody other than Emily who liked them.

Tonight she was sitting at her desk looking at a textbook, but she glanced up with a smile when he walked in.

He sat on the edge of her desk and began flipping through a stack of DVDs for lack of anything better to do.

Emily was always trying to get him more interested in her anime movies, but he found them too obscure, with whole casts of characters he didn't understand, and he liked teasing her. "What is this thing?" he asked with wonder, pointing at a saucer-eyed pink animal on one of the DVD covers. "Why does it have to look like its eyes are going to pop out of its head?"

"Because people like characters that look a lot, but not too much, like humans," Emily said patiently. "The people who make those movies have actually studied this. They call it the uncanny valley."

"The what?"

"The uncanny valley," she repeated. "It's a graph that shows how people respond to characters or robots better the more human they look, but once they become too much like humans, people get grossed out because they look like dead bodies or something. That's why people like this stuff"—she waved at the DVD he was holding—"more than they like, say, the people in that movie *The Polar Express*."

"Well, I still think they're crazy-looking," he said, putting the DVD back on her desk.

"You play video games," she replied. "Like those aren't filled with completely random characters."

"Yeah, but you don't have to care about them; you just shoot them."

"You're such a guy," she said, and laughed.

"How can you say that? I'm pretty much the only guy you know."

"That's not true." She put her book down.

"Name one other guy you hang out with regularly. One."

"Nick," she shot back.

"He's your cousin!"

"So what? He's still a guy."

"Also, he's nine."

"And even more so what? He plays video games and rides his bike around just like you do. You're practically the same person." She laughed again.

"Okay, fine, you win," he said, laughing too. "I'll give you your nine-year-old cousin Nick whom you see twice a year when his family visits from Virginia. Name another."

She paused. "Well . . . there's Aidan."

"Who's that?"

She dropped her eyes and fussed with the DVDs on the desk, aligning them neatly. "He works at the stationery store in Red Mill."

"Oh."

Emily waited, like she expected him to say something else. When he didn't, she stood suddenly.

"Actually I don't even know his last name," she said. She dumped the pile of DVDs messily into a box next to her bed and went back to her chair with a frosty stiffness.

"So, how about Andrew Marks leaving?" he asked, to change the subject.

"I'm glad he's gone," she said. "Totally obnoxious."

"I know, but you realize what that means?"

"You knew it would happen eventually, right? I mean, everybody else left," she said. "But I guess it must be weird to be the last boy."

Jeremy sank onto her bed. "It's more than weird; it's a disaster. It's only the beginning of seventh grade. I've got two more years of this! That's . . . three hundred seventeen days," he said. "Three hundred seventeen days, three hundred seventeen million opportunities for total humiliation."

"Wait, did you just do the math in your head?" she asked. "Dork."

He ignored her. "Three hundred seventeen days, give or take a sick day. Maybe I'll get lucky with the flu and be out for a week." He flopped back on the bed.

"You could get mono," Emily offered. "I hear it takes you out for like a month."

"Great! So I'm supposed to be wishing for a month sick in bed?" he said. "I hate my life."

"Don't say stuff like that." Emily turned around in her chair and looked at him, her tone serious. "It's not that big of a deal unless you make it one."

"How would you like to be the only girl in a school full of boys?"

"That would be different."

"How?"

"Because boys are . . . gross," she said. "Besides, you've been going to this school since kindergarten, you have plenty of friends, and you get really good grades. And it's a prestigious school. Not to mention your mother would never let you switch."

"My mother would never be able to pay for me to switch—that's the problem," he said.

"It's more than that. I think she likes having all of you kids together. It makes her feel safe."

"Thanks, Dr. Phil."

"I'm serious!" Emily said. "Anyway, you can't do anything about it; you just said so yourself. So stop, like, focusing on how horrible it is. That's my advice."

"So, basically, suck it up and deal?" He sighed, but he knew she was only attempting to help. At least Emily tried, in her way, to listen to his point of view.

"No, not exactly. But you could stop complaining all the time and try to be happy."

"Well, maybe that's the point. Maybe I'm tired of complaining, and I want to do something to *make* myself happy instead of just going along with what everybody else wants."

Emily peered at him. "You're not planning on doing anything . . . bad . . . are you?"

"What, like running away?"

"No. Something stupid that will ruin your whole entire life, like flunking out."

"Why would that be stupid?" he asked as innocently as possible. "If I went to a place like Harding I'd get straight As without even trying."

"But straight As at Harding don't mean the same thing as straight As at St. Edith's. At least not to prep schools. Besides, your mom would kill you." She got up and walked over to the bed but didn't sit down. "Let me guess, Claudia Hoffmann and those other girls in the Film Club are putting you up to something? I wouldn't put it past them to convince you to get kicked out for laughs."

When she talked about Claudia and her friends, Emily's voice sounded more like a teacher than a kid their own age.

"They didn't put me up to anything. I haven't even talked to Claudia about any of this yet except for five seconds on the bus. And I'm not planning anything, anyway." He stood up. "I just came over to ask what we were supposed to read for social studies. I forgot to write it down."

"Okay," she said, giving him an injured look. "I didn't mean to make you mad. I'm sorry."

"I'm not mad!" But the way it came out sounded like

he was. "Sorry, I'm really not. I have a lot on my mind."

Emily pulled out her Hello Kitty day planner and consulted a page, then wrote something down on a heart-shaped sticky note and handed it to him. "Those are the chapters."

"Great," he said.

She didn't reply, and he was about to get up and leave, but then she said, "Hey, do you want to watch a movie or something Friday?"

"Oh, I can't. Claudia's having people over, I think. You should come," he added unconvincingly.

Emily snorted and said in her most prudish voice —the one the other girls liked to imitate—"I don't think so."

"It's just a bunch of people watching a movie. It'll be fun."

But she'd turned back to her book. He suddenly had the sensation he was supposed to say or do something else, but he didn't have the first clue what. So he edged toward the door.

"I gotta go. My mom's making dinner, and she'll be mad if I'm late. See you tomorrow."

# FOUR

**THE NEXT MORNING CLAUDIA AND JEREMY MET** on the steps of St. Edith's like they usually did on Film Club days. Having a few minutes before morning assembly gave him the perfect opportunity to share his list of ideas with her—he'd flattened it out again after dinner—and his plan to get expelled.

"I can't stand it anymore," he said. Claudia was leaning against a pillar, waiting for him. "All I keep thinking about is the amount of time I'm going to spend being the only guy around. 'Five hundred twenty-five thousand six hundred minutes'? Isn't that how the song goes?"

"If you start singing show tunes, so help me, I will bash in your head with a pipe."

"It's from *Rent*! Not, like, *Les Miz* or *Annie* or something."

"I don't care," Claudia said.

Claudia was determined to be a director when she grew up. A *movie* director—that was an important distinction. She had no interest, only contempt, for the theater, which was one of the reasons why she wasn't very popular among the drama crowd. "Do you really think I want to spend my life teaching people how to use jazz hands while they sing about Oklahoma?" was the way she put it. "As if."

"Anyway, what are you trying to say?" she asked. "That you're running away from home? Quitting school? You always say stuff like that, but we both know you don't really mean it."

"No," he said quietly. "I want to find a way to get kicked out. And I need your help."

Claudia's take on the news was, as expected, kind of intense.

Her first reaction was denial. "Ha-ha, very funny, Jeremy," she said. "You're a regular riot this morning."

Next came anger. "What the heck is wrong with you? Here I was, thinking this was going to be a great year, we're going to have so much fun, and all you care about is yourself. I hate you."

Up next was bargaining. "Can't you at least stay one more year? Just to see how it goes. You hated Andrew Marks anyway, so it's not some great loss. And we're going to have such a good time. I know this year's movie is going to be great; I just have to find the right script."

Depression: "This stinks. I can't believe it. My best friend wants to get expelled and leave me all by myself. I wish I'd never gotten out of bed this morning. How could you do this to me?"

Then, when it was almost time for them to go inside for morning assembly, acceptance.

"Fine," she said. "If this is what you want, I'll help you come up with a plan. You're my best friend, so it's the least I can do." She sighed, like the weight of the world was on her shoulders. "But whatever we do, it has to wait until after we figure out the Film Club project. I've got too much on my mind right now."

Jeremy had only joined Film Club because Emily had talked him into it a couple of years ago. But it was where he'd met Claudia, and it had become his favorite thing about school.

There were two parts of Film Club: watching and making. Twice a month after school the group got together to watch a movie and discuss it. Claudia tended to dominate these discussions, but Jeremy didn't care. It was a nice way to watch movies, on a big screen in the auditorium. Emily started the trend of bringing popcorn, which made it even better.

The second part of Film Club was more complicated. It involved actually making movies. And while Claudia was one of several outspoken voices in the selection and discussion of films in the movie-watching part of the club, she was the undisputed queen of the production end. In fact, Film Club had only been about watching movies until she campaigned to make them too. A large donation from her parents to purchase equipment hadn't hurt.

Claudia didn't need the equipment—she had an excellent camera of her own and a top-of-the-line computer to edit with. What she needed was manpower.

"Minions," Jeremy called them.

"Manpower," Claudia corrected him calmly. "Or womanpower, if you like that better. Because the only way to make the kind of film that gets me noticed is with a real, live crew."

And somehow, every semester, she got legions of classmates—girls who had probably never expressed any interest in filmmaking before—to stand around holding lights, spend afternoons running cables and making props, and generally follow orders just so they could be attached, however minimally, to the project.

It was a source of great bitterness among the drama geeks that so many more people wanted to be in the Film Club movies than the annual spring musical. The drama kids had even petitioned successfully to keep the film project in the fall so that the two wouldn't overlap, but still, more people went out for film than for drama every year. Something about the glamour of Hollywood—and, probably, of Claudia—as well as the comparative lameness of the other extracurricular offerings at St. Edith's made even the most menial job on one of the films a hot ticket.

Casting was another story entirely. For every girl who wanted to be on the movie crew, there were a dozen who wanted to be the star. But while being in the movie was a major goal of almost everyone involved, Jeremy was the only person guaranteed a part, because finding a script to suit a school with only one boy was a major headache.

Mr. Reynolds's sole requirement was that they work from an existing script or story. So unless you could convince girls to play Hamlet or Charlie Brown, the pickings were extremely slim. Even the stories with female lead characters, like *The Diary of Anne Frank*, had multiple male parts too. In kindergarten and first grade, when they'd had class plays, many girls had happily played a boy part if it meant a bigger role. But somewhere around sixth grade that changed.

In fact, what they should have been discussing at that afternoon's Film Club meeting was suggestions for this year's script, since auditions needed to happen pretty quickly and they still hadn't chosen anything. Even Claudia, normally so opinionated, was at a loss.

But instead when the club met in the library, the main topic of conversation was Andrew Marks. As it had been ever since the news broke the day before.

All day Jeremy had had the distinct impression that everyone was hyperaware of his lone-boy status. He could feel the eyes on him, judging him, even more than usual. But at Film Club most of the girls thought he was being an idiot for even caring.

"It's not like you were even friends with him," Delaney pointed out. She was tall, with long hair she flipped around like she was in a shampoo commercial.

"If you cared that much about guy friends, then you

should have at least tried to be nice," Tabitha said. "Maybe he was just shy?"

"We all know Andrew Marks was a jerk," Jeremy said with little patience. They didn't understand that it wasn't about guy friends, it was about all the little daily humiliations, and how they added up to the point where he wondered how he could stand it.

"What about Billy Franklin, then? He was cool. And you always treated him like he was a clown," Delaney offered. Billy Franklin, number eight, had moved to Boston at the end of last year.

"He *was* a clown; you just thought he was cute," Tabitha said to her.

"I can't help it. You know how much I like boys with blue eyes," Delaney replied, and a couple of the other girls nodded in agreement.

Jeremy made a strangled noise. "Stop it, okay? Just stop." There were few things he hated more than when the girls talked about boys as though he, an actual boy, wasn't sitting right there.

Claudia wasn't participating in the conversation. Instead she was poring over some books of plays and stories. "Can we stop talking about Andrew Marks and think about important stuff, like what movie we're going to make this year?" she finally said. "I don't want to end up doing *Annie* like stupid Reynolds suggests every week."

Emily shot her a look, even though Reynolds wasn't there yet.

"I can't wait to go to high school," Claudia said. "Think of all the great movies I'll get to make. Anything I want. I could get people to write them for me. Or do scripts that have tons of guys without worrying. Like *Twelve Angry Men*. Or *The Deer Hunter*."

At least Film Club was the one place at St. Edith's where being a boy was a distinct advantage, because Jeremy always got to be the star. Of course, most of the roles he would have really loved to perform were in plays that were impossible to mount in a school that was 99.999 percent women. Most of the time Claudia just picked things and assigned him a role. He didn't even know why they made him try out, but he knew better than to argue with a gang of amateur filmmakers.

Other schools, real all-girl schools, sometimes recruited boys from other institutions to play key roles. Drama-loving boys and aspiring actors would go on auditions from Miss Whatever's Academy for Girls to St. Sophia's. One boy— Jason Monroe was his name—had starred in shows at girls' schools from Belchertown to Lowell.

But St. Edith's was technically coed thanks to Jeremy and, up until this week, Andrew. So they never managed to interest any outsiders in their productions.

Claudia stood up and dramatically swept the books off the table and into her arms.

"I can't work like this. I have one guy and a billion women who won't play boys," she said. "Don't you people realize it is next to impossible to find a movie that has at least two women in it, talking about something other than a guy? Don't you want to fight that kind of . . . of . . . social conditioning, or whatever you call it—"

"The Bechdel test," Emily said suddenly.

"What?" Claudia was thrown off her rant for a second.

"You're talking about the Bechdel test," Emily said, and then catching the quizzical looks around the table, continued. "It's, well, a test obviously. Of movies. To see if there are at least two women having a conversation that isn't about a man. A lot of movies, even really great ones, fail. Including the entire original Star Wars trilogy, by the way," she added, shooting a pointed look at Jeremy.

"Whatever," Claudia said. "I'm going to go to the library in town to read plays and look online. I'm going to find something tonight if it kills me."

She shoved the pile of books and papers into her backpack, stood up, and stalked off.

"Aren't you going to check those out?" Jeremy called, but she was already clomping her way out of the library, triggering the stolen-book alarm and setting the librarian after her.

# FIVE

**THE NEXT DAY IN MORNING ASSEMBLY CLAUDIA**
was tired but jubilant.

"I found it," she whispered to Jeremy before Powell
began the announcements. "I found our movie. It's a little
out there, but it's got tons of parts for everyone, and even
special effects! And I have the whole script, so we don't
even have to adapt anything. It's this sci-fi television show
I found at the comic book store. It's going to be unbeliev-
ably awesome."

"Great," Jeremy said, only half listening.

"Don't you know what this means?" Claudia asked
even more insistently. "We can get started on your plan.
Our plan. You know?" She gave him a sharp look.

"Oh," he said, perking up. "So you're really going to
help me get kicked out?"

"Shhh!" she practically hissed. "What's wrong with
you? Do you want to get caught before we even do anything? Besides," she continued in a more normal whisper.
"Of course I'm going to help you. I said I would, didn't I?

We'll talk about it after school at Mickey's, once I hang up the posters for auditions. Emily promised to make them after lunch."

Mickey's was a roadside café and convenience store halfway between school and Jeremy's house that catered to both locals and tourists. It was great as long as you didn't look too long at the plates or worry about flies. Jeremy didn't care about that stuff, mostly, but even so, he never ate any of the pastries from the open tray.

Both he and Claudia liked Mickey's. Claudia said it was "real" compared to the upscale cafés most of their class-mates went to after school. Jeremy mainly liked it because it was cheap.

He was buoyant for the rest of the morning. Even though they had no real plan yet, he felt like for the first time he was actually taking action to improve his lot in life instead of just sitting around complaining.

At lunch he stopped to talk to Emily near the cafeteria doors. He was going to ask about the posters, but Claudia and Delaney approached carrying trays and Emily's mouth formed a sour pout.

"Hey, Jeremy. Hey, Auntie Em," Claudia said.

Jeremy shot her a look. He hated when Claudia called Emily that.

"Sorry," Claudia said breezily. "It's the outfit."

"You guys are wearing the same uniform!" he said to her.

Up until fifth grade the girls at St. Edith's wore light-blue-and-yellow plaid jumpers over white shirts. If it was cold, they had baby-blue cardigan sweaters with the school crest on the chest. The older girls wore wool skirts in the same plaid pattern, white button-down shirts, and V-neck sweaters. The boys—well, Jeremy— wore the same shirt-and-sweater combo, but with navy dress slacks and a plaid tie.

The choice of color for the slacks had been filled with drama when boys were first admitted to St. Edith's. A faction of the board felt the boys should wear light blue pants, but another group thought the chance of the color not matching the sweater was too high. A smaller but still vocal minority was in favor of plaid. The worst idea, and a favorite of the director at the time, was for the boys to wear gray pinstriped three-piece suits, like an army of pint-size lawyers. Thankfully, at least to Jeremy, that idea never got past the suggestion stage.

But even he had to admit Emily's prim sweater and shirt, buttoned to the very top, looked very different next to Claudia, with her patch-covered backpack and bright orange tights. He was surprised she hadn't been called to the office already today. Dress code violations were her specialty.

"Thanks for being a jerk, Claudia," Emily said.

"Oh, come off it, Emily. I was just being sarcastic." As usual, what passed for humor with everyone else came off differently when Emily was the target.

"Well, maybe next time you can ring a little bell so I'll know," Emily replied dryly. It was the kind of thing Jeremy thought was funny, that he wished she would say more around people like Claudia. "I'll see you later. I've got to get started on those posters," Emily said to him, and left.

"Oh man," Delaney said with her trademark hair flip. She turned to Jeremy. "That girl is too much. You do realize she's totally in love with you, don't you?"

"That's moronic," Jeremy said. The idea of Emily thinking of him in that way made him cringe.

"Is it? I was thinking 'pathetic' might be a better word,"

Delaney said as the three of them made their way to their favorite table near the back.

"Delaney might have a point," Claudia said, dumping her backpack on the table. "I think you just don't want to admit it. Maybe it'll feel too much like you're using her."

"I'm not using Emily for anything. We're friends; we've been friends forever."

"Right," Delaney said with a knowing nod. "Sure."

After the final bell Jeremy went to find Claudia at her locker. But she barely noticed him approach. Instead she was staring at a piece of paper in a state of obvious and intense indignation.

"This?" she was saying. "Really?"

She talked like she was surrounded by people, but it was only the two of them.

"Just . . . just . . . look," she said, and thrust the paper at him. She was at a loss for words, a real rarity with Claudia.

He looked at the paper in his hands. It was the poster Emily had made advertising the auditions for Film Club. *Captain Flynn and the Mission to Mercury* was apparently the name of the script. If Claudia had mentioned the title in morning assembly, he didn't remember. The poster said the time and place of the auditions and seemed fine, as far as he could tell, written in some sort of bubbly lettering surrounded by clip-art balloons. There were maybe a few more exclamation points than he would have personally used, but beyond that he didn't see what was wrong with it.

"What's the problem?"

It was the wrong thing to ask.

"What's the problem? What's the problem?" Claudia almost yelled. "Do you even see this thing? It looks like the invitation to a little kid's birthday party, not the opportunity to participate in the cinematic event of the year!"

Jeremy figured Claudia was overreacting about the design of the poster and immediately stopped caring. He put on a fake concerned face and said, "Well, at least people will know about the auditions."

"But they'll probably think they're trying out for a revival of *Bye Bye Birdie*," Claudia grumbled. "I'm just going to take a deep breath and be calm. I'm not going to give Auntie Em the satisfaction of knowing her evil plot to destroy me almost succeeded."

She took the poster from him and jammed it violently onto a nearby bulletin board.

Jeremy was pretty sure Emily hadn't deliberately designed the posters to drive Claudia crazy . . . or maybe she had. That was a provocative idea. But there were more important things on his mind.

"So you said we'd go to Mickey's?" he ventured.

"Oh, right," Claudia said, nodding. "The plan."

She gave him her cloak-and-dagger smile again, and he knew the storm had passed for now. "We need to come up with a name for it. Like Operation something."

"Operation Get Jeremy Expelled?" he suggested.

"Shh," she said, looking around quickly. "Too obvious. We need something . . . more mysterious."

"Right," he said. "Well, why don't you tell me what you're planning, and then I can come up with a name that's mysterious enough for you."

But she wouldn't tell him anything, not until they had walked all the way to Mickey's, with Jeremy rolling his bike along. A kid they called Whitey was outside as usual, fussing with the newspapers in the rack out front, like he was organizing them. Or maybe stealing one. Jeremy was never sure.

Claudia had given him the nickname. They didn't know the boy's real name, and he looked, well, white, with very pale skin and almost white hair and eyebrows so light it was like they were missing. At the same time he seemed kind of tough, like he should be hanging out on a street corner somewhere in New York City, not in front of a sad little diner in the middle of nowhere.

Whitey greeted Jeremy with a nod and a hopeful sounding "Hey! What's up?"

"Hi?" Jeremy said back. He never knew what to say to this kid. Did he, like, live there? He probably went to the public school, where the hours were different. And maybe he lived in the trailer park tucked among the trees across the street, the one most people thought was for tourists on a budget but Jeremy knew really wasn't. Travelers and retirees stayed at the Spruces Trailer Park, which had an entrance like a fine resort with stone lions and a fountain. The nameless park across from Mickey's didn't even have an entrance, just a driveway of gravel and weeds.

The boy didn't say anything else, so Jeremy and Claudia went inside and placed their order. Quasimodo, the guy who ran the place, handed over their drinks in his usual painstaking and wordless manner. Warm sodas in cans and translucent plastic cups half filled with ice.

They called him Quasimodo, like the Hunchback of Notre Dame, but he didn't have a hump, technically. He was just always hunched over something—the cash register, where he pecked out prices, or the ancient meat slicer or a magazine he kept hidden behind his forearm. They didn't know what his real name was, just that it definitely wasn't Mickey. They'd heard him correct enough people.

"So, before we start, I need to make sure you're serious about this," Claudia said. Her voice took on a professorial tone. "Is it true you are lacking in positive male role models at St. Edith's now that Andrew Marks has finally transferred?"

"You sound like one of those books my mom has on her nightstand," he said. His mother's bedside table was full of books about divorce and children of divorce and raising boys after a divorce. A whole pile of books, all with the same words in the title, just in a different order.

"The thing is, have you ever considered that the problem isn't that there aren't enough guys around? Maybe it's you. Maybe you like girls better," Claudia said.

"I thought you came here to help me get kicked out of school, not to lecture me on why I should stay," Jeremy said impatiently. She didn't understand how long he'd feared this moment, how every single boy who had ever gone to St. Edith's dreaded being what he had become.

"Well, maybe you could use some guys around for companionship," Claudia mused. "But I could argue you're already a jerk, so what's the point?"

"Claudia, I'm serious!"

"Serious about getting kicked out of school? Well, okay," she said. "But you have to promise me you'll stick around long enough to film your scenes for the movie. Though getting you expelled should take a couple of weeks, at least, so we'll be able to get those done if we can get everybody else moving."

"Great." Jeremy was trying to be patient. "I just need to get out of there as soon as possible."

Claudia always did this, stalled around a question before she actually came out with what she thought. It was annoying and wouldn't have been worth it except he knew she, of all people, was the one person who could actually invent a plan that would work. And of course she knew he knew, which is why she was being like this.

Finally she made her pronouncement.

"Are you ready to have your mind officially blown?"

He nodded.

"Then I have one word for you," Claudia said. "Pranks."

# SIX

**"PRANKS?" JEREMY ASKED. "COME ON, CLAUDIA,** be serious."

"I am serious. Serious as a heart attack."

"You mean practical jokes?" Jeremy was confused. "Wedgies, gluing people's lockers shut, stuff like that?"

Claudia shot him a withering look. "Leave it to you to think small. No, I'm talking about major pranks, on the whole school, the kind of thing people will be talking about for years."

"So you mean like mooning everyone at an assembly? I don't think I'd really be able to pull that off."

"That's not a prank; that's just being an idiot. I'm talking about smart pranks, funny things."

"Oh, hacks," Jeremy said. "My dad did stuff like that in college. One time they even put a police car on top of the main dome—"

Claudia cut him off. "As much as I'd hate to interrupt one of your fascinating stories about your father, I was just getting to my point: I think you need to come up with some pranks to play at school. Correction, I think *we* need to come up with some pranks to play at school, and you can take the credit—or the blame, really—because I don't think you'd be able to come up with anything as good as I would. No offense, but I don't think you have the right . . . cinematic mind-set."

He let the dig pass. "And why pranks?"

"Because it'll get you in trouble but not arrested or sent to reform school. We don't want you to get in actual trouble, just enough so that they ask you to leave. So you can't set fire to the building or anything."

"Set fire to the building?" Jeremy was alarmed. He had been joking when he'd put that idea on his list. He didn't think Claudia would take it seriously.

"I said, you *can't* set fire to the building. Are you even listening? I mean harmless pranks, but annoying things, things that'll upset Powell and the other suits and get you in a decent amount of trouble. Enough to get you expelled."

"Okay." He had to admit, the idea had merit. It was definitely better than anything he'd come up with. "I can see that. But what?"

"I'm not sure," she said. "I have to think about it. And since we're an all-girls school—"

"An almost all-girls school," he interrupted.

"Almost all-girls school," she repeated, "with no history of prank making, we're going to have to get creative. Why is that, by the way? Why don't girls' schools do pranks the way boys' schools do? Or is it just St. Dither's that doesn't do anything fun?"

"You've never pulled any pranks before," he pointed out.

"Well, that's something we're about to fix," she said firmly. "Anyway, I was thinking first we need to test the waters, come up with some easy pranks, things that might get us in trouble if we're caught but not expelled. I want to see how upset they get."

"Okay," Jeremy said. It seemed impossible to imagine him, Jeremy, doing pranks that would have the whole school buzzing. But maybe it was exactly the thing he needed.

"And remember, I'm not getting caught! You're the one who wants to get expelled, not me," she said. "It'll be an experiment. To find the perfect prank to get you kicked out. May take some time, but you'll be at a new school by Christmas. We just have to come up with our first big idea."

Jeremy thought for a minute. "Maybe we should go to the library?"

"The library? We're about to embark on a life of crime, trying to get you kicked out of school, and your first thought is 'Hey, let's go do some research in the library'?" She made a face at him. "You have serious, serious issues."

"I'll talk to my dad then," he said. "Like I was trying to say, he did all sorts of pranks in college. Hacks, he called them." Spending twenty minutes listening to his dad talk about algae blooms and melting glaciers might be worth it if he got a brilliant idea for a prank in exchange. He caught Claudia's eye. "Don't worry, I won't let him know what we're up to. I'll just pretend I'm interested in hearing about his glory days at MIT."

"Fine," Claudia said. "Just try not to give away the whole thing before we even start, okay? Because I really think this is going to work, if we do it right. We might even be able to pull the first one this weekend."

# SEVEN

**THAT NIGHT WHEN HIS MOM GOT HOME, JEREMY** told her he wanted to talk to his father.

This was always a tricky proposition. In theory, his dad was supposed to call once a week, but due to his crazy saving-the-world-on-a-solar-powered-boat schedule, he usually forgot. Which made his mother upset, which made Jeremy pretend he didn't care so she wouldn't feel bad, which made her resigned, which made him feel weird asking.

This had gone on long enough that Jeremy acted like he didn't mind if his dad called or not, never asked to call him, and just stayed sort of vague and noncommittal when his mother got it in her head he needed to reach out to his father on his own.

But that night he took a deep breath and said, "Hey, I want to call Dad later. Is that cool?"

"Why?" she asked suspiciously. Then, before he could answer, she continued, "Oh God, listen to me, asking why my son wants to talk to his father on the phone. I can't believe myself. Of course you can call him; call him whenever you want. I don't even know why you're asking permission. Do I make you feel like you have to ask permission to talk to your father? You can tell me the truth."

"No, of course not," Jeremy said, but she was still looking at him. He realized she wanted him to answer the question, even though she also wanted to pretend she hadn't asked it. "It's something for school. I was reading about . . . dolphins."

"Really?" she said, and then laughed. "Well, good, I guess. Ask your father about dolphins. Just don't ask him about when he's coming to visit or where his child support check is or anything, you know, important, because whatever he says will be total fiction. But dolphins, that he'll know all about."

She paused. "Wait. Forget I said that. I don't want to bad-mouth your father; he's your father, after all. And he loves you very much." She looked suddenly weepy. "And so do I," she said, zooming in for a hug.

Conversations like this were precisely why Jeremy didn't like discussing his father with her. But he just escaped from her arms and went into the kitchen to dial the seemingly endless number of his father's satellite phone, which was written on a piece of paper stuck to the wall under layers of Scotch tape. His boat could be anywhere in the Atlantic, so the satellite phone was the only way to reach him.

It had been so long since he'd lived with his father that he had no clear picture of him anymore, just a swirl of memories. The sandpaper scratch of his beard when he kissed Jeremy good night. His loud, honking laugh. How he didn't flush the toilet after he peed because he thought it wasted water.

"Wow, dude, what a fantastic surprise," his father said when he answered the phone. "It's been way too long since I heard your voice, kid."

He sounded the same as always, totally relaxed, like he was lying on a beach somewhere. Which he could have been, for all Jeremy knew.

"Yeah," Jeremy said.

"I'm so glad you called, champ." His dad used these forced nicknames when they spoke, like they had an easy rapport filled with "sport" and "buddy" and "guy" instead of an arm's-length relationship marked by occasional phone calls and two-months-late birthday presents postmarked from somewhere Jeremy had never heard of.

"Did you get any snow yet? Because by the time you're my age snow probably won't exist except in laboratories and at the top of the Himalayas, so you better enjoy it while you can."

"No, no snow," Jeremy replied. Typical Dad. He was always more interested in the rising sea levels than whatever was going on with his kids.

"Anyway, I had a great day," his dad continued. "I finally fixed the engine, and we even saw some North Atlantic right whales. They were awesome. Did you know they're one of the most endangered species of whale in the world?"

Jeremy knew that once his dad started talking about his boat and his inventions and his scientific work, any opportunity to ask about pranks would be lost. "Dad?" Jeremy started, hesitant. "Can I ask you something?"

His father seemed distracted by something on the boat but said, "Sure. Anything."

Jeremy lowered his voice and took the phone to the back door so his mother, hovering in the hall, couldn't hear. "Remember the pranks you did in college?"

"The hacks? Oh yeah," he said, and chuckled. "There's

a long history of that at MIT. Did you hear about the upside-down lounge they did a few years ago? All the furniture hanging from the arch at the Media Lab. Even a pool table! One of my buddies e-mailed me about it. Of course, there were always rules about never hurting anyone and only doing things that could be fixed. That was really important. Anyway, what about them?"

It was now or never. If he were caught and got in trouble—which was technically what he wanted to happen—he hoped his dad would never remember this conversation. Or maybe that he would and feel guilty about not being around when Jeremy embarked on his life of crime. He pushed that thought to the back of his mind.

"Well, I was just wondering if you could tell me about some of the ones you did, all those stories about police cars on tops of buildings and things. I mean, how did you get it up there? The police car? Or what about the one with the cast on the statue? That was kind of cool. And wasn't there one time when the guys dressed up as referees and blew whistles and fed the seagulls before the Harvard-Yale game? How did you come up with that idea?"

Jeremy's dad paused. A long pause. When he spoke

again, his voice sounded different. "Well, you might have the wrong impression, buddy."

"What do you mean?"

He paused again. "It's just that . . . when I say 'we' did hacks, you know, I meant the students at MIT. Not me specifically. Just the kids there. Other kids. Did you think I was one of the hackers? That's pretty wild."

"What?" All the times Jeremy had heard those stories, he'd thought it was his dad doing this stuff, sneaking out at night, coming up with creative craziness. Figured it was all just a stupid lie. "I thought . . ."

"I'm sorry, sport," his father said, "if you got the wrong idea. I just . . . I just wasn't . . . that kind of kid in college. I liked the hacks and everything, but I wasn't actually doing them. I don't even know who did them, honestly. There were always rumors. . . . I remember there was this guy in my dorm, back when I lived in Bexley . . ."

He started another story about crazy engineer and scientist hijinks, but Jeremy wasn't listening. Clearly, his dad was going to be no help. Jeremy was disappointed but not really surprised.

So now it was up to him and Claudia.

He called her after he hung up with his dad, this time from his room on the cell phone he was only supposed to use "for emergencies." He definitely didn't want his mom to overhear this call.

"So?" Claudia asked. "Did you talk to him?"

"Yeah, and he was pretty much useless."

"And you're surprised?"

"Not really. But he did tell me one thing—pranks have to have rules."

Claudia snorted.

"I mean it, Claudia," Jeremy said. "I don't want anybody actually getting hurt."

"Fine," she said. "Why don't you make one of your lists if that'll make you happy?"

"I already did." He'd scribbled it out while his dad was going on about sea turtles, and now he read it to her.

THE RULES OF PRANKS
Nobody gets hurt
Nobody gets humiliated
Nothing is permanent
Nothing is broken

"Okay, fine," she said, when he was finished. "We'll follow your rules. As long as we follow the most important one. Number five: All pranks must be epic."

A smile slowly spread across Jeremy's face, even though Claudia couldn't see it. He was beginning to think this might be really fun. "Of course. Anyway, when are we going to start?"

"Sunday," she said. "I've already got an idea."

"You do? What is it?"

"Not telling," she said placidly. "Not until I work out the details. I have to talk to my brother."

"Your brother? Why?"

Claudia's brother, Ian, was a senior at St. Anselm's, an all-boys school in Red Mill. Jeremy had met him dozens of times, but Ian always stared at him like he was some kid who'd wandered in off the street.

"You'll see," she said. "I'll talk to him tonight. Just be ready to meet me late Sunday. Like nine or ten."

"Wait," Jeremy said. "How am I going to get out that late on a school night? My mom'll freak."

"I don't know. Tell her you have to study."

"With you? At ten o'clock?" They both knew his mother would never agree. An image of her saying "Do you think I was born yesterday?" came into his head.

"Well, tell her it's with Emily or something. And we'll make it 8:30, okay?"

"I don't know," he said. It wasn't like his mother would object to him going over to study at Emily's, even on a school night. But it felt a little bit like that was—what had Claudia said?—using her.

"Well, you'll come up with something," she said. "Just be ready."

He had a sudden pang of guilt, thinking about how mad his mother would get—how disappointed she would be—when he was expelled from St. Edith's. But he couldn't focus on that.

Because at least now they had a plan.

He tried to picture himself going to a coed or all-boys school, walking in the door, saying hi to a bunch of guys. Going to classes where he wasn't the only boy in the room. Maybe doing that fist-bump thing guys do? Or did people only do that in movies?

What he really wanted was to just be normal, fit in, be one of many. It would be amazing, he thought. Worth getting expelled, and worth every bit of screaming and door slamming his mother could muster.

The only thing he had to do first was pull off a few pranks.

# EIGHT

**SUNDAY NIGHT AROUND EIGHT JEREMY WALKED**
into the kitchen as calmly as possible.

"Mom," he said. "Can I go to Emily's? To do homework?"

"It's getting late . . . ," she began, glancing at the clock.

"I know, but I really need her help. We have a Spanish test coming up."

"Well, okay." Jeremy's Spanish grade had been down last year. She looked closely at him. "But don't stay out too late. And call before you walk home."

"Of course." He felt a little sheepish, like he always did when he knew she was worrying.

When he arrived, Emily was in the den with her dog, watching *Kung Fu Panda*. She had a thing for martial arts, pandas, and Jack Black, so the movie was pretty much a slam dunk for her. She didn't seem surprised to see him.

He nodded hello and sat down. He didn't really need help with his Spanish homework. And the test wasn't until next week.

"That's the Wilhelm scream," Emily said. She had

scooted over on the sofa, but he hadn't noticed she was right next to him until she spoke.

"What?"

"The Wilhelm scream. It's one of the most famous sound effects in movies. Listen." She stopped the DVD, went back a few frames, and played the scene again. A white tigerlike creature threw someone in the air, who screamed.

Jeremy arched his eyebrows at Emily.

"Come on, you've heard that scream a million times, in a million movies. *Star Wars. Lord of the Rings.* Even *Aladdin*! That's why it's famous. It's like a cliché, you know, for people who do sound effects."

"That's really interesting," he said, grabbing a handful of popcorn from the bowl on Emily's lap and leaning back on the sofa.

"There's another one you hear all the time too," she said, not yet turning the movie back on. "It's a thunder sound; it's in all sorts of movies, mainly horror. I'd love to get it as a ringtone or something."

"Where do you even learn this stuff?"

"Around," she said. "I read about it, in books and online."

"So why's it called that? The William scream?"

"Wilhelm," she said. "It's named after a character in a movie, one of the first movies it was in. Sometimes it's called 'man eaten by alligator scream.' I kind of like that name, but it doesn't make sense in something like *Star Wars*."

He looked at her admiringly. "Maybe you should be the one directing movies in Film Club, instead of just doing the posters."

She shrugged. "I dunno. Just because you like something doesn't mean you want to do it as your job. I think I like being a fan better."

She picked up the remote like she was going to start the movie again but didn't.

"Anyway, why are you over here on a Sunday night? It's kind of late, isn't it? Or do you have questions about the homework?"

Emily always fretted about homework and spent two or three times as long as required on each assignment. Jeremy didn't understand why. She got good grades, but he basically got the same grades she did, even without copying and recopying the problems on fresh paper or highlighting the answers with a different colored pen.

"Nah, I've done everything except study for Spanish," he said. "And I can do that next weekend."

Emily looked worried. "But we've got that test coming up. I've been studying for days."

"Well, maybe I can look at your notes tomorrow?" he said, grabbing more popcorn.

Emily's highlighted, color-coded, Post-it-marked, and cross-referenced notes were the stuff of legend at St. Edith's. She probably could have sold them for fifty dollars a page come finals time. But she let Jeremy look at them for free. Sometimes. She shook her head ruefully, but she was smiling. "Jeremy Miner, what would you do without my notes?"

"I don't know—I'd probably have to start taking notes myself," he said truthfully.

"And Lord knows we wouldn't want that." She laughed and patted the dog, then looked up with a mischievous glint in her eye. "So, my mom got some wasabi peas at Trader Joe's. . . ."

He didn't answer but glanced at the clock on the wall. Claudia should be calling any minute now. For a brief flash he wondered if he really wanted to go with her at all. Maybe it would be better to just stay here with Emily—talking and watching movies, giving poor trusting Princess Di random food items—and forget the whole plan. But he knew that wouldn't solve anything.

As expected, his phone rang at eight thirty on the dot. "We're down the street," Claudia whispered when he answered, though she really didn't have to. "Come as soon as you can."

Emily was staring at him as he ended the call. He hadn't planned this part, the part where he explained why he was leaving. "So, hey, I was just stopping by. To talk about school and stuff."

Her eyebrows lowered, but she said nothing.

"So, I like, really need to go, but um—thanks for telling me about that scream thing; that was really interesting." He was talking too fast, he knew, and it made him sound guilty, but he couldn't help it. "And we can maybe hang out after school tomorrow and study, right?"

She chewed on her lips. "Right," she said, pressing play on the remote again. "I'm not even going to ask what you're up to," she added, almost under her breath. "I honestly and truly don't care."

"It's nothing, really. I just have to get home," he said, not looking at her. "So, bye?"

She didn't respond.

Jeremy walked out of her house and down the street to where Claudia's brother Ian's Jeep was idling by a fire hydrant. He had reluctantly agreed to be their driver for this clandestine mission.

"That took long enough," Claudia said impatiently as Jeremy climbed into the backseat. Ian was sitting at the steering wheel looking as though he had never been so bored in his life.

"Well, I had to say good-bye and everything. I couldn't just walk out. Are you going to tell me what we're doing now?"

"In a minute," Claudia said. Jeremy could barely hear her over the music Ian was playing. "Wait till we get around the block."

"But what about—?" He jerked his head toward her brother.

"Oh, it's fine," she said. "Ian doesn't care what we do. Besides, I promised to write his next English paper."

Ian pulled the car away from the curb before Jeremy

had his seat belt on. "Turn here," Claudia yelled at him. "And slow down."

Ian slowed the car to a crawl, and Claudia turned off the music.

"We have to be quiet or it won't work," she said, and leaned over the front seat to talk to Jeremy. "Come on, I scoped out a few targets on our way over."

# NINE

**"SEE THAT HOUSE OVER THERE?" CLAUDIA WHIS**-pered to Jeremy. They were standing on a street Jeremy had never been down before. It was chilly and the sky was dark, but streetlamps cut paths of light through the gloom. Some of the houses were decorated for Halloween.

"Sure," Jeremy said, peering into the dimness. This part of Lower Falls was nicer than his neighborhood, with ranch houses and small colonials set close together on quarter-acre plots. The houses were well cared for, and people paid a lot of attention to their gardens.

"See the gnome?" Claudia asked.

"The what?"

"The lawn gnome, Jeremy, the little man," she said impatiently.

He could make out a ten-inch-high statue in the shadow of the front hedges. He nodded. "Okay, what about it?"

"Do I have to spell everything out for you?" she asked. "We're going to take it. Come on."

Claudia began walking slowly down the sidewalk in

front of the house with her head down like she was looking for something on the ground. Then she darted across the lawn, grabbed the ceramic creature under one arm, ran back to the street, and tossed it into the back of Ian's Jeep, which was still idling by the curb.

"Now it's your turn," she said.

Jeremy wasn't sure what the point of all this was, but if he knew Claudia, there definitely was one. So he began to scan the houses.

*There*, he thought, spotting one. This house was dark too. He slowly walked up the front path as though he lived there and at the last minute veered onto the lawn, grabbing the statuette of a fat man with a long beard and a pipe.

He sped back to the car, tossed the gnome on the back-seat like Claudia had, and looked around quickly to make sure no one was watching. The street was still deserted. The only motion was the flickering light of television sets in living rooms and the wind moving through the trees.

Claudia gave him a thumbs-up but shook her head when he started to get into the car. "There's more," she whispered.

"Okay," he hissed back, and walked farther down the block, faster than before. Another house, this time with several lawn ornaments—a spinning fabric pinwheel in rainbow colors, some ceramic frogs, a small faux wishing well, and in the corner, a gnome, this one with a fishing pole.

He did the same thing as before: strolled up the walk as though he meant to go into the house, then ducked down, because these people were watching TV in their living room. He crossed the lawn in a crouch, grabbed the gnome, and headed quickly back to the Jeep.

"I think there were only three on this block," Claudia said. "Get in, we'll go around the corner. I scoped it out this afternoon; there are tons of them, at least a dozen. Then we'll bring them to school."

"Bring them to school?" Jeremy asked. "But how are we going to return them to their owners?"

Claudia looked a little disgusted.

"We have to give them back, right?" he said. "We can't just take them for good. I thought you agreed to the rules, Claudia. Nothing permanent, nothing that can't be fixed."

"You're really not cut out for this, are you?"

"I just don't like stealing. Is that so wrong?"

"Fine," she said. "I have some masking tape in my

backpack. We'll write the addresses down and stick them to the bottom of each one. But disguise your handwriting, because that would be a royally stupid way to get caught."

The next hour was spent collecting gnomes from all over town. Jeremy had never noticed how many people seemed to like this kind of lawn ornament, but they were incredibly popular. At least Claudia had paid attention; she remembered seeing gnomes in all sorts of places. There seemed to be at least one on every block. After forty-five minutes the Jeep was so crowded Jeremy couldn't fit without sitting three or four of the figurines on his lap, like silent bearded children. Every time Ian hit the brakes, china clanked all around them and Jeremy's heart lurched.

Slowly they progressed through Lower Falls into Red Mill and toward St. Edith's Academy, until they made their final theft, only three blocks from the school.

This was the closest call. Someone must have heard Jeremy, because as he reached the sidewalk with his treasure, a man wearing nothing but a pair of sweatpants came to the front door.

"Hello? Is anybody there? Hello?"

Hiding the gnome behind his back, his heart thumping, Jeremy edged toward Ian's Jeep, parked in front, and leaned against it like it was the most normal thing in the world. Behind him a pair of hands reached through the open car window and grabbed the gnome.

The man at the door peered at Jeremy. "Can I help you?"

"Nope," Jeremy gulped, hoping the man couldn't see the dozens of china figures in the car behind him. He was glad he'd grown about two inches over the summer.

"Get in," Claudia hissed, and Jeremy gave the man what he hoped was a casual wave and complied. Once he was in the car, he started laughing like crazy, in big heaving breaths. His heart was racing faster than if he'd run around the block at top speed.

"This is insane," he said when he could finally talk.

"But awesome," Claudia replied, laughing too.

When they got to St. Edith's, Claudia directed her brother to pull his Jeep around back where a driveway led to a small loading dock used for the cafeteria. It was the only part of the parking lot that wasn't visible from the street.

"I'm staying in the car," Ian said. It was the first time he'd spoken all evening.

Claudia and Jeremy worked quickly, carrying rotund figures back and forth under each arm, and then silently slipped back to the car. Ian reversed out of the loading dock without putting on his headlights, like a driver in a thriller movie. Nobody spoke until they were a couple of blocks away from school.

"So," Claudia said. "Wanna come hang out for a while? My parents are in New York for the weekend, and Ian won't care."

"I can't," Jeremy said. "I told my mom I was going to Emily's house, and she's going to expect me home any minute. Actually, I'm supposed to call her when I'm headed back, so she'll probably be watching out the back door. You need to drop me off on Emily's block."

"All right. But we both have to be at school early tomorrow so we can see the reaction."

"Are you sure the janitor isn't going to get rid of them when he opens up the doors in the morning?"

"Elmer?" Claudia laughed. "He won't do anything

that's not on his list of regular chores unless Director Powell specifically tells him. Remember when we tried to get him to move some tables for Film Club last year? We practically had to get an executive order before he'd even touch them. He'll probably think it's some sort of school-spirit display, or something."

"If you say so," he said.

She gave a gleeful little laugh, surprisingly giggly for Claudia. "I can't wait to see Powell's face."

# TEN

**THE NEXT MORNING THE STUDENTS AND FACULTY**
of St. Edith's Academy arrived to face an army standing at
full attention in front of the school.

It was an army of little men, some with beards and
many with tall, pointed hats. Some had fishing poles,
others had wheelbarrows, and one, inexplicably, held a
frog. As Claudia had predicted, Elmer the janitor had
done nothing about the gnome invasion without orders
from the school director.

In the morning light there seemed to be far more of
the knee-high figurines than Jeremy remembered putting
out the night before. Dozens of eerie little men silently
eyed them in the slanting fall sunshine.

Students arrived in buses, in cars, and on foot. Most
mornings they were loud and hurried, rushing to get to class
before the first bell. But this morning the pattern changed.

Instead of plunging ahead, the students slowed down,
their voices quieting, until they finally came to a stop on the
sidewalk in front of the school, staring at the little figures

dotting the lawn and the path and the steps as if it were a real army barring their entry. A few let out soft giggles. Others looked worried. Most stood silent and confused. A couple people pulled out cell phones and began taking pictures.

Around the time the mass of students began to out-number the gnomes staring back at them, Mr. Reynolds arrived. His blue Toyota slowed as he drove past the school, then sped up and quickly swerved into the faculty parking area. He strode toward the nearly silent group of spectators.

"What is going on here?" he asked, and without wait-ing for an answer stormed up the path, mowing down gnomes as he went.

Once he'd disappeared through the heavy oak doors of St. Edith's, the spell was broken. Slowly students began to enter the building one by one or in pairs. They followed the path Mr. Reynolds had taken to avoid knocking over any more gnomes themselves.

Jeremy hung back with Claudia. She was quivering as though she could barely keep herself from jumping up and down. He was trying not to look at her, but he could still sense her glee. "Look at them," she whispered. "They don't have a clue. This is classic."

Jeremy's stomach felt like it was made of solid lead and pumped full of air at the same time. He felt very aware of himself standing there, but none of the people rushing past even looked at him. To them he was just regular, everyday Jeremy: dependable, studious, a little bit awkward.

But now there was this other Jeremy, the one only he knew about. (Well, he and Claudia.) The kind of boy who snuck out at night and pulled crazy stunts. It was like having a secret identity. He only wished he'd been the one to come up with the idea for the prank, and he made a mental note to rectify that in the future.

He knew they could get in trouble for this. Serious trouble. People yelling at him, pointing fingers in his face, his mother screeching and then crying when she realized he might be expelled. But as he stood there, in the rush of his success, none of that mattered.

He felt invincible.

Then Ms. Powell arrived.

Jeremy pretended to examine the gnome nearest him but watched Powell's movements out of the corner of his eye. She parked her car in her reserved spot in the parking lot, but instead of taking the direct path to the front door, she walked slowly around to where the students were standing, taking in the whole view.

He glanced up at her; he couldn't help it. And he was surprised to see a strange expression on her face. It wasn't anger, as he'd expected. It wasn't surprise or consternation or even fear. It was something more strategic and calculating than that. Like she had just gotten a very big idea.

He had no clue what to make of it.

"Come on," Claudia said finally. She was still bouncing on her heels, but girls were trickling into the school. As new people arrived, they gaped and moved on, picking their way through the pint-size crowd. None of the gnomes had been disturbed except for the half dozen Reynolds had knocked down. "We'll be late for morning assembly, and I really want to get a good seat for this one."

They walked inside, toward the auditorium at the rear of the building. Morning assembly was normally a subdued affair, with students yawning behind their hands and writing notes to friends as classmates spoke about how many slots were open on the chess team or the details of the next Earth Club retreat, and the director offered words of wisdom or sometimes warning.

But today the room had an energetic hum, with girls milling around and talking excitedly as Jeremy and Claudia walked down the aisle to the second row from the front. Nobody but teachers ever sat in the actual front row. Few people ever even sat in the second, unless they were giving a presentation. But today Claudia wanted to be front and center.

When Powell walked in, later than usual, her arms were crossed across her chest. The students were still whispering, but most of them sat down quickly and looked at her with an unusual level of interest.

Nobody knew what to expect. This kind of thing was unprecedented at St. Edith's. There had never been any sort of pranks before. There hadn't even been fights, unless you counted a hair-pulling incident from five years before that was still talked about as an epic event. There wasn't graffiti in the bathroom or gum under the desks. It just wasn't that kind of school.

"Well, well, well," Powell said after she stepped up to the podium. She had short, gelled hair and dark-framed glasses. The entire auditorium stopped speaking at once. "It looks like we have a band of merry pranksters in our midst."

Jeremy and Claudia looked at each other, but Jeremy glanced away as fast as he could. If anyone with any sense had looked at Claudia at that moment, they would have known she was guilty. Not because she looked guilty—not at all. She looked absolutely delighted.

Jeremy didn't know what he looked like. Probably like he wanted to vomit.

But then Powell allowed herself a small smile.

"Now, girls," she said, and Jeremy grumbled internally despite himself. "I know this kind of thing seems like it's amusing, but we have to behave more responsibly in the future. I believe those lawn ornaments outside were taken from homes in town, and I'm pretty sure our neighbors are not going to be happy about that. That's not being good citizens."

The way she said it made it sound as if even if the neighbors weren't happy, in some way she was. It was mystifying.

"I know, I know; students like to do this sort of thing. Let's face it. This isn't the first school I've worked at, and I've seen far worse. So I'm willing to turn a blind eye this one time." At first she seemed to be trying not to smile, but then her voice became serious. "However, I fully expect that the student or students responsible for this will make sure to return these little . . . characters"—here the student body tittered—"to their rightful homes as soon as possible."

A girl Jeremy didn't know raised her hand.

"Yes?" Powell said.

"What if it wasn't one of us? What if it was, like, another school that did it?"

"Or townies," the girl next to her added.

Powell glanced at the girl and considered. "Well, then I suppose I'll have Elmer collect the gnomes and put them somewhere. I really do think we should at least try to return them."

Reynolds, who was sitting on a chair behind the podium, stood and whispered something to Powell, who clapped her hands and spoke to the students again.

"Apparently the, ah, items all have addresses on the bottom. So we'll be able to get them back to their owners with no harm done."

Reynolds looked horrified.

"Besides the obvious misbehavior, of course," Powell said, again with the corners of her mouth twitching.

"But"—and here she addressed the whole room again—"I want all of you to know that while I'm not looking to punish anyone this time, we do need to keep this kind of mischief to a minimum so it doesn't interfere with the most important part of our work here at St. Edith's, our studies. Okay?"

There were murmurs of assent around the room. Jeremy and Claudia gaped at the director.

"Moving on," she said, shuffling some papers. "I believe the debate team wanted to make an announcement. Miss Stephens?"

As a tiny girl with glasses made her way toward the stage, Claudia shook her head. "I don't believe it," she said, loud enough that people nearby looked at her. Jeremy stuck his elbow in her ribs. She didn't speak again, just sat perfectly still for the rest of the assembly, in stark contrast to her high energy moments before.

Afterward, as they walked out of the auditorium toward their first class, Claudia was still subdued. "That was so weird," she said finally. "Not what I expected at all. It was almost like . . . kind of as though . . . she—"

"Liked it," Jeremy finished for her.

"Yeah," Claudia said. "Very strange. And I think this means you're definitely not going to get expelled for this one."

"Right," Jeremy said. For a moment he had forgotten that was the plan. It had been lost in the weirdness of the morning.

"We'll just have to come up with something bigger," Claudia said.

Jeremy nodded. He felt conflicted. When Powell had smiled and brushed off their crime, he hadn't been dismayed, like Claudia. Instead he'd felt relieved, like he'd just missed being hit by a speeding train. But it had also been thrilling, like he'd gotten away with something really huge.

It seemed almost a shame to try to get caught. But he knew that was what he had to do if he wanted to get kicked out of St. Edith's.

That night at dinner Jeremy's mother rehashed the entire incident in her own inimitable way. "I can't believe she's not doing anything to try and stop this garbage," she said. "If Hutchinson"—the old director, from before the disastrous football season—"had been here, these kids would have been found out and expelled. I didn't always approve of her tactics, but at least she got results." (Truthfully, she had complained as bitterly, if not more so, about Director Hutchinson as she did about Powell.)

"*This* one"—and the way she said it spoke volumes—"seems to think the 'buzz' generated by this kind of thing is good for the school. Can you imagine? That it attracts students! She even brought up that horrible website the girls talk about—"

"Girls and boys," Jeremy interjected.

"Oh, don't be so sensitive; it's not all about you. I'm just talking. But okay, that nasty rag the girls and boys all talk about, the *Prep Confidante*?" she faltered.

"Confidential," Jane said, and they all looked at her. "What? Abby's sister reads it."

"Right," their mother said. "Well, in the staff meeting, she said this kind of thing would improve our rankings on that stupid blog! She even gave them an interview when they called to ask about the prank! Lord only knows how they found out, but to actually talk to them? This is what we get, hiring a corporate robot in a suit as director."

Jeremy's mother stabbed at her potatoes with a fork.

"Can you imagine? She said students at most other schools play pranks, and some even have a whole history of them. Like a special prank day, organized and everything. And that maybe it would be good for us to have this kind of thing going on. She's completely lost her mind."

Jeremy was listening intently but trying to pretend he wasn't so as not to arouse his mother's suspicions; she was always skeptical when her kids were too attentive to her ranting. And he wasn't so sure Powell was crazy. It was true the *Con* mocked St. Edith's because it didn't have any of the fun, crazy traditions that other schools did, so maybe Powell was right. Maybe people would think St. Edith's was a cooler place if there were more pranks.

A year ago he might have been pleased. Anything to improve the school's dismal reputation and maybe keep other boys from leaving. But now he realized Powell's attitude was going to make his job a whole lot harder. He wondered what kind of prank they would have to pull to actually get into trouble if Powell was considering the one they had just pulled a benefit.

Because playing pranks was the only plan they had.

⇨

# PREP CONFIDENTIAL

**RED MILL, MA:** Will wonders never cease? The *Con* has news to report about St. Edith's School for Girls and the Occasional Unfortunate Stray Boy that isn't about placing second in a knitting championship. Apparently, someone (or someones; as of press time it remained unclear) at the school has decided to shake things up a little, with a recent school-wide prank that had dozens of garden gnomes stolen from nearby homes and set up on the lawn. The prank itself only gets a B for originality—we think the boys at St. Anselm's do this one at least once a year (they call it "gnoming")—but an absolute A for audacity, considering the source.

Director Amanda Powell even gave an interview to the *Con*. After we made sure it wasn't a practical joke, we picked ourselves up off the floor and listened to what she had to say.

"While we don't condone stealing, and all the figurines will be returned to their owners, we do encourage a spirit of creativity and enthusiasm here. This particular act may have been a little bit misguided, but it shows that St. Edith's is just as much fun as any other school in the northeast."

There was more, mainly about some sort of committee, but we stopped listening after the "just as much fun" part.

Still, bravo, St. Dither's. There may be life in the old girl yet!

# ELEVEN

AUDITIONS FOR CLAUDIA'S MOVIE—BECAUSE REALLY
the movie was hers more than anyone else's—began the
following week, and they got off to the usual start: a room-
ful of girls, plus Jeremy, being bossed around by Claudia.

Auditions were always exhausting. Unlike everyone
else, Jeremy had to be in the room the whole time so he
could read the same lines over and over with a parade of
girls trying out to be his costar. He had to admit getting so
much positive attention from girls started out as exciting,
but after about the tenth round it became a little grueling.
The girls always stared at him like he had just fallen out
of the sky, even though he'd gone to school with most of
them since kindergarten.

This time, however, it was different.

Because there was a new girl.

This was unusual enough at St. Edith's. Practically
everyone there had started in the first grade. Instead of
coming to the school, people usually left, either by trans-
ferring or graduating.

But it wasn't just that this girl was new. It was the way that Jeremy noticed her. The kind of noticing where you somehow know you're never going to stop noticing that person, no matter how many times they walk into a room.

The members of the Film Club were gathered in the band room, and Jeremy sat on the closed lid of the piano watching Claudia work her magic. She was wearing her glasses, which she only wore in public if she was trying to look extremely serious, and carrying a clipboard.

"QUIET, EVERYONE! I CAN'T HEAR MYSELF THINK!" she hollered, far louder than any of the chatter in the room. Half the people fell silent. The other half laughed and went back to their conversations. Mr. Reynolds looked up from his crossword puzzle briefly, surprised Jeremy by shooting him a quick grin, and looked back down.

And that's when the new girl walked in.

It wasn't like there weren't plenty of girls around. The place was jam-packed with girls. Girls doing homework in chairs under the window. Girls sprawled on the floor talking to friends. Girls peeking around the doors from the hall and texting on contraband cell phones in shadowy corners. The entire place was crawling with girls, except for Jeremy and Mr. Reynolds.

Girls with long hair and girls with short hair. Girls who beat him on every test and girls in danger of flunking out. Girls who played sports, sang in the choir, wrote tortured poetry, and lived with their grandmothers. Tall, short, pretty, not really pretty, and too pretty. Every kind of girl. He'd been surrounded by them for years. So he wasn't sure why out of all of them, this was the one he had noticed. But he had.

The girl was slim and on the short side with long brown hair. She went up to Claudia, who barely looked up from her clipboard. Jeremy strained to hear the new girl's voice.

"I'm here for the auditions? For the movie?"

Every phrase sounded like a question, and Jeremy could see from the shape of Claudia's mouth that she had noticed. Claudia thought people who talked that way were tentative and insecure. *No stage presence*, she would write on her clipboard.

"Give me your name and take a seat."

"Anna?" the girl said. "Anna Macintosh?"

Claudia wrote on the clipboard, then again on a little

piece of paper and handed it to the girl, who sat down by the window. She turned away from Jeremy to talk to another girl, which gave him a chance to look her over.

It wasn't that she was prettier than the other girls (she was definitely pretty, but so were a lot of them), but there was something about her that made him want to talk to her. He wondered what it was going to be like auditioning with her playing the opposite part.

He quickly counted to figure out how many girls had showed up to audition before this girl—Anna, she'd said her name was. Thirty-three.

"Everybody, I need your attention," Claudia said, clapping her hands loudly. "I've given you each a number. Now I'm going to ask you all to leave this room and either go out into the hall or the main lobby. When it's your turn, someone will come and call out the number that's being auditioned, but if you don't come when your number is called, you'll have to wait until the end, okay?"

Most of the girls grabbed their stuff and slowly filed out. The Film Club members stayed behind to help with the audition process, including Mr. Reynolds, who put down his crossword a little reluctantly and sat in the chair next to Claudia. "Ready to head into the fray, Mr. Miner?"

Jeremy nodded and hopped off the piano. Showtime.

"So, you read the scene I gave you, right?" Claudia asked him.

"Sure," he lied.

"Okay, well, stand here first"—she waved at a piece of tape stuck to one of the squares of vinyl flooring—"but then when it's time to go and she stops you, cross here, to the space dirigible." She pointed to another piece of tape.

"Space dirigible? What is that, some kind of space-ship?" Tabitha said from the other side of the room. "We can't build a whole spaceship!"

Claudia sighed impatiently. "It's going to be special effects, okay? I've got it all figured out."

Delaney, sitting on the floor, flipped through her own copy of the script, her eyes looking more incredulous with each passing page. "Okay," she said as unconvincingly as possible. "Whatever you say."

Claudia stopped what she was doing and turned. "Can't we try something different for once?" Her voice got louder so the rest of the Film Club, scattered around doing various tasks, could hear. "Do you guys really want to do the same old thing every year? Or do you want to try something that could be really groundbreaking?"

Nobody said anything.

Claudia sighed. "Fine," she said. "I guess I'll just have to follow my own vision, as usual."

She turned back to Jeremy. "If I don't stop the scene by the time we get to the part about the humanoid monkeys, then walk to the front and we'll finish up there."

"Right," Jeremy said, only half listening. He was wondering about that girl. Number thirty-three. Anna.

Unfortunately, it took hours for them to even get into the twenties. By that point Jeremy was spending the time between each candidate flopped down on a row of plastic chairs staring at the overhead lights in a dull trance, while Claudia and Tabitha, who had been anointed assistant casting director, held hushed conversations at the little desk in the corner. Mr. Reynolds began sneaking back to his crossword between each candidate.

In the scene they were using for auditions the male lead, astronaut Captain Flynn—played by Jeremy, naturally—was leaving in his space dirigible to get some supplies from a dangerous new planet. He and his potential love interest,

Dr. Zizmor, were arguing about their plot to take over the world. And something about alien monkeys and evil plants. It didn't make a whole lot of sense to Jeremy.

"But you said you'd stay. No matter what," Dr. Zizmor was supposed to say.

Some of the girls screamed this line. Some of them said it completely flat. One girl said it as a question and was immediately cut off and sent packing by Claudia.

Jeremy's next line was "I know what I said! But those alien plants are vicious, and someone has to stop them."

He felt moronic even saying this, but he tried to make it seem powerful and important. Something a leading man would say.

Still, it was all garbage. In the lulls between auditioners, Jeremy asked Claudia, "Where did you find this script again?" at least ten times an hour.

But her only answer was "Sixteen female parts, one male part. I work with what I've got."

And it just grew later and later.

Jeremy wondered if the new girl had given up and gone home. Some people did, because they were going to miss their ride or they had to be home for dinner—if auditions went past six, Reynolds would order pizza, but a lot of people didn't know that—or they assumed one of the other girls had already gotten the lead.

Number twenty-eight didn't show up. Neither did number thirty. The closer Jeremy got to his audition with the new girl the more anxious and irritable he became.

Number thirty-one was nervous and slow, pausing over every word, until Jeremy ended up screaming his line—"I know what I said"—so loudly that she almost burst into tears.

Finally Claudia sent Tabitha out into the hallway to call number thirty-three.

"Anna, right?" Claudia said. She was tired, so her tone was curt, but Jeremy hoped it didn't sound discouraging. "Here," she said, and handed Anna a script. "This is Jeremy. He's playing Captain Flynn, and he'll read with you."

He'd read these lines with lots of girls, but this felt different. He was suddenly hyperaware of his posture and of the way his hair stuck up around his ears.

"Hi, I'm Jeremy," he said a little squeakily, for lack of anything better to do, then mentally kicked himself. Claudia had just said that.

"Hi, Jeremy," Anna said back, and smiled—a huge smile, bigger than you'd expect for an on-the-small-side kind of girl, but it suited her.

"Well, I usually stand here." He pointed at a tape mark on the floor. "And then Dr. Zizmor, that's you, stands here." Another tape mark. "But we're not too worried about the blocking right now. Do you want to take a minute to look over the scene before we start?"

"I've read the script," she said. "I know this scene pretty well."

This was new. Most of the girls stumbled, reading the scene for the first time. He was always the one who knew it by heart. And this girl sounded a lot more confident with the script in her hands than she had seemed earlier.

When they began, he felt conscious of every word he was saying, despite having performed the scene over two dozen times. Toward the end he was supposed to yell at her. But as he bore down with the line "You'll see! I'll be the only one alive!"—she was shorter than he was, which was cool, since so few of the girls who auditioned were—he felt, to his horror, little bits of spittle flying out of his mouth.

She turned away, and he was aghast that maybe he had

actually spat on her, but when she turned back she was still in character. "Fine! Go build your boat. And when the space monkeys come, the rest of us will be safe in my dead father's tower and you'll be all alone on the ocean!"

She quizzically glanced toward Claudia after she said that line. Jeremy understood that look. The more he read the script the crazier it seemed.

"But the aliens are allergic to salt water!" Jeremy spat back (hopefully not literally). "They'll never catch me!"

"Oh, Marcus," Anna said. "Please . . . What if it's true? What if they've finally built that agony beam . . . ? Everything we've created will be destroyed. . . ." Her eyes shone as she looked at him, and for a minute Jeremy forgot they were acting.

In fact, looking at her, he felt more like he'd been pitched headfirst down a well.

"Meredith, I'm sorry. Come with me—it's the only way," he stammered.

She shook her head.

"And scene!" Claudia called out. "Good, very good. Thank you very much, Anna. We'll let you know Monday."

Jeremy blinked and suddenly remembered where they

were. He'd never really thought about acting before, beyond saying the lines right and trying not to look like an idiot. But it was clear Anna could actually act. Even Mr. Reynolds seemed to pay more attention to this scene than the others and said, "Nice job, kids," to the pair of them.

Anna smiled at Jeremy, collected her backpack, and headed out the double doors. Jeremy watched her without wanting to seem like he was watching, silently hoping Claudia saw what he saw and would cast her.

That night he had trouble falling asleep. Things he'd said and done during the day, especially at the auditions, kept passing in front of his eyes and making him cringe all over again. He supposed other boys sometimes agonized over things they said to girls at school, but other boys didn't have every single thing they said at school be to girls. He squeezed the pillow around his face and ears to try to block it out, but the memory of auditioning with Anna kept creeping in. Why had he said hi in that crazy voice? And he was completely convinced he had spat right in her face.

Honestly, if it weren't for the audition, she probably wouldn't even have noticed him at all, except as the one pathetic boy in the whole school. And now she probably thought he was lame, being in Film Club. She probably liked guys who played sports—boy sports like football and basketball. Or maybe guys who were in a band. Or failing that, a guy in the school band. He felt a prickle of guilt about his dusty French horn, which he hadn't touched since last year when he convinced his mother he had to quit band in order to focus on his studies. Maybe he should pick it up again?

Somehow Jeremy didn't think a girl like Anna would be impressed by a guy who played third-string French horn in the school stage band, especially not one whose last report card said "tries hard despite lack of discernable talent."

Of course, nobody knew the secret Jeremy, the one who snuck out at night and pranked the whole school, the one who was more than just the only boy in the room. But he wasn't even sure if that was the real him or just another part he was trying to play, like in Claudia's movies.

That was why he needed to get out of St. Edith's.

Because maybe, just maybe, if he got the chance to have a normal life at a normal school, he could be himself. Not just what everybody else saw.

# TWELVE

**THE FOLLOWING MONDAY AFTERNOON CLAUDIA** hung up the cast list on the bulletin board outside the band room. Jeremy was the male lead in the movie, of course. The astronaut who was trying to build a ship or a boat or fight the aliens, or something. Honestly, for most productions he didn't even look at the cast list, he was so sure who would be on it. But this time he tried to be casual as he peeked over Claudia's shoulder.

That girl, Anna, was playing opposite him: Captain Flynn . . . Jeremy Miner. Dr. Meredith Zizmor . . . Anna Macintosh.

He didn't look at anything else on the sheet, just turned away with a small smile. He'd finally read the whole script, as convoluted as it was, and there were definitely some romantic parts. Maybe instead of being the weird guy in a school for girls, for once he could be the strong, capable guy. An action guy. The kind of guy who gets the girl. At least on screen. Maybe a girl like Anna would be impressed by someone like that.

After school Claudia and Jeremy went to Mickey's to hash out an idea for a new prank. They sat at his least favorite table, the one right by the counter with the short leg that kept tapping on the floor every time he moved his elbow. Claudia seemed to take Powell's reaction to the Gnome Incident as a personal insult, or at the very least a call to arms.

"We've just got to come up with something better" was her constant refrain.

Jeremy thought about Anna and wondered if she'd seen the cast list yet. Obviously, she wouldn't care that he got the opposite part; they barely knew each other. Maybe she was even a little bit disappointed it was him instead of some other guy. Not that there were any other guys to choose from at St. Edith's.

He wondered what she would think if she knew he was behind the gnome prank. It would be hard to ignore him then.

But telling her would be like Batman sitting Catwoman down over a cup of coffee and explaining he's actually just Bruce Wayne and that he made all those great gadgets in his basement workshop. Where was the mystery in that?

He eventually had to force himself to stop thinking about Anna and listen to what Claudia was saying, which was, actually, "Are you even listening to me?"

"Yeah, yeah," he said.

She growled at him. "This is really important, and you're just, like, spacing out."

"I'm sorry." He tried to focus on her, but now Whitey was hovering in that irritating way people do when they want to be part of something but, well, aren't.

Every time Jeremy's eyes moved in his direction, Whitey perked up, almost hopefully, like he thought Jeremy was going to talk to him. So Jeremy started to feel like he needed a blinder on that side, forcing him not to look in order to avoid the awkwardness. Of course, that only made him feel like he *had* to look.

"I'm sorry," he said, probably for the tenth time. "So, what were you saying?"

"I was SAYING that we need to come up with an idea for a better prank," Claudia said.

"Well, it can't be one where I have to go to Emily's again."

Claudia rolled her eyes. "Like I care."

"I'm serious, Claudia! There's no point in pulling a bunch

of pranks if we get caught before Powell cares enough to expel me. And Emily is totally suspicious; I'm sure of it."

"But I don't see how we can do anything if you can't get out of your house at night."

A voice came from behind him. "You could say you were going to the film festival in town."

Jeremy was so surprised he froze. But Claudia stared over his shoulder at Whitey.

"What?" Jeremy finally said, half turning, but not really looking at the kid.

"There's a big film festival over the next two weekends. You could say you had to see one of the movies for school. It's an easy way to get out of the house."

Claudia nodded slowly. "That might work. I totally forgot about the film festival"—a lie: Claudia boycotted any film festival that wouldn't show one of her films, which meant all of them—"and I think they're showing some movie about the Civil War this year. You could say it was for social studies."

"No, that's too complicated. It'll never work," Jeremy said with more force than he'd planned. "We just have to come up with something else, something we can do during the day."

Whitey looked a little crestfallen, but all he said was, "It was just a suggestion."

Jeremy avoided looking at Whitey, who retreated to the corner of the café by a busted arcade game.

He didn't know why he didn't want to use Whitey's idea. Maybe because this was supposed to be something he and Claudia were doing, and he didn't want this strange kid butting in. Because there wasn't anything really wrong with Whitey, and the kid was just trying to help, even if he was inexplicably irritating.

But Jeremy had more important things to think about.

Like coming up with a plan for the second prank. As good as Claudia was at this sort of thing, he really thought he should be the person to come up with something big. He was the one trying to get kicked out, after all. As much as he racked his brain, however, he couldn't think of a single great idea.

"Powell did give me one idea," Claudia said slowly.

"Okay. What?"

"Well, you know how that girl asked what would happen if the prank was done by another school?"

"Yes . . ."

"Well, what if *we* pranked another school?"

He shook his head, not comprehending.

"What I mean is, how would you like to get a little revenge on the jerks at MacArthur Prep?"

"You know," he said eagerly, "at MIT they dressed up as referees days before the big Harvard-Yale game and stood on the field and blew whistles and then fed the seagulls. So when the first whistle blew at the game—"

"Seagulls?" Claudia said, making a face. "When was the last time you saw seagulls in Red Mill?"

Jeremy's face fell. "Okay, fine. What's your big idea then?"

"I saw pictures of something on the Internet—I think from France? I just have to see if I could get into the supply closet at my dad's college. We'd need about a million Post-it notes."

"Post-it notes?" He stared at her in wonder.

"Yeah, sticky notes, you know, little papers with glue on them. Everybody uses them."

"I know what Post-it notes *are*, Claudia; just what are we going to do with a million of them?"

She smiled her broadest smile. "I told you. Revenge."

# THIRTEEN

**THE NEXT THURSDAY, JEREMY WAS STANDING** outside St. Edith's in the early evening darkness holding a brick of Post-it notes as thick as a phone book. One by one he handed them to Claudia, who stood on a step stool next to a school bus that was slowly changing from yellow to pink, purple, and red, square by square.

"It looks great," he said, "but won't they blow away? Maybe we should have done it from the inside." Claudia's idea was brilliant, as usual, and he wished he'd been the one to come up with it. *The next one*, he promised himself. *The best one.*

"And break into the bus?" she said, not exactly patiently. "I checked the weather; it'll be fine. Besides, the whole point of using Post-its is that they won't damage anything. Remember your rules?" He couldn't see her eyes, but he was pretty sure they were rolling.

Of course he remembered the rules. He'd annoyed Claudia enough when he'd insisted on following them by not stealing the Post-it notes from her dad's office. She had reluctantly agreed to buy them at the stationery store downtown. It had taken all of Jeremy's birthday money and half a dozen trips at different times of day so the store clerks wouldn't get suspicious. But now they were finally standing outside St. Edith's during a volleyball game against MacArthur Prep, Jeremy handing up pieces of paper and Claudia sticking them in place, occasionally referring to a sketch tucked into her pocket.

Suddenly they both froze.

Voices came from the doors at the rear of the school. Jeremy and Claudia were hidden by the bus but close enough to hear every word.

"Are you sure you can walk home?" a voice said. It was a girl's voice, vaguely familiar. Someone from their school. But was it someone who would tell on them?

"Yeah, it's only a couple of blocks," another girl's voice said. "I just really feel like I'm going to puke."

"Okay," the first girl said. "Text me when you get there, though."

Footsteps passed the bus, then faded. Jeremy held his breath until he heard the soft click of the door closing again. He let the air out in a slow, long whoosh. There was that crazy roller-coaster rush again. His heart was pounding so hard he could hear it, and his stomach seemed to have moved a foot from where it belonged. Even though he knew the plan was to eventually be found out, the feeling of almost-but-not-quite being caught was a little addictive.

"That was close," he said. "I thought you said nobody comes out here until the final point is scored."

"Well, they don't usually," Claudia said irritably, grabbing more Post-it notes out of his hand. "We just have to hurry."

Ten minutes later they were finished, and they stepped back to admire their handiwork. "Not too shabby," Claudia said. It was an understatement.

"It's awesome," Jeremy said.

Claudia pulled a small camera from her pocket and started filming.

"What are you doing?" Jeremy hissed.

"Just getting a little footage," she said calmly. "It might come in handy. Don't you want proof it was you?"

He had to admit she had a point.

After Claudia filmed the bus for a few minutes, they hid the step stool in the bushes by the parking lot and quietly reentered the gym, where the undefeated St. Edith's was clobbering MacArthur. They slowly climbed up into the bleachers, trying not to attract attention, and scooted down until they were mixed in with the rest of the crowd.

"Where were you?" Emily said from behind Jeremy. "Rachel just scored like, three times, and you missed it."

"You sound like my mother."

"If I was your mother I'd clock you on the side of the head for missing your sister's match" was Emily's retort.

"No you wouldn't! My mother believes in nonviolence, remember?"

She laughed. "Fine. Point taken."

After the final point had been made —St. Edith's won, naturally—and the girls (and Jeremy) had cheered loudly, people slowly trooped outside to their parents' cars and the waiting buses. The MacArthur Prep team would probably shower and change first, but most of the students who had come along to cheer them on left the school right away. Claudia dug her nails into Jeremy's arm as the first students made their way around the MacArthur team bus.

"What the?" A boy said loudly. It was the same boy, Mike, who had hassled Jeremy at the last match. He probably had a sister on the team, like Jeremy did.

"What are you talking about, Mike?" another boy said, coming around the side of the bus.

Then: "WHOA . . ."

Their voices drew others, and soon a big enough crowd had gathered that Jeremy and Claudia felt comfortable sauntering around the bus to gaze at the results of their work.

It was a huge picture made entirely out of Post-it notes. A bright red pair of lips and a tongue sticking out—Claudia had found the directions on the Internet—and then words, in pink and purple: "St. Edith's Rules!" ("A little trite, but sometimes that's the most effective," Claudia had decided while they were planning it.)

Giggles, then a whistle came from a gang of St. Edith's girls. A girl in Rachel's grade started a slow clap. Delaney, the most jaded of Jeremy's friends, looked astonished, and even some of the MacArthur kids had smiles on their faces and poked one another. But the adults in the crowd were clearly not amused.

One of the MacArthur chaperones walked slowly up to the bus, peeled off one of the notes, and then looked at it in his hand like it might explode.

"Where's the headmaster?" he finally said in a loud,

angry voice. "And Director Powell? I think they both need to see this."

"Maybe we should get out of here," Jeremy whispered to Claudia.

"And miss all the fun? No way."

Jeremy felt antsy and nervous. He suspected that however amused Powell had been by the gnomes, she would probably view the pranks differently when they made other people—other powerful people—upset.

And he was right. As Powell and the headmaster from MacArthur Prep approached the bus, he could hear her trying to placate him, her voice growing louder and higher as they came closer.

"Really, I don't know what's going on. I can assure you no harm was—"

"I don't care what you put up with at your school, Amanda, but trust me, we don't stand for this kind of tomfoolery at MacArthur. I know what's been going on at St. Edith's. I read the *Con*."

"Yes, but really, it's just—"

"No, it's not just," the headmaster interrupted as they rounded the corner and stepped through the throng of students to the front of the bus. "Is this how you treat guests at your school? Is this what you teach your girls?"

*And one boy,* Jeremy thought fruitlessly.

For a second it looked like Director Powell was suppressing a smile as she took in the bus. But when she turned back to the headmaster, her voice was as grim as his. "Clearly, students were loitering in the parking lot during the game, which is expressly forbidden," she said. "As is, obviously, committing vandalism against the MacArthur Prep bus."

The MacArthur headmaster grunted in assent.

She turned to the crowd, which had become silent and still. "I'm not going to stand for this kind of behavior. Tomorrow, at morning assembly, I want to know who is responsible for this." She paused and let her eyes wander over the collected students. "And this time, I mean it."

# FOURTEEN

**THE NEXT DAY MORNING ASSEMBLY BUZZED EVEN** more than it had the day of the gnome prank. "Who do you think it was?" Jeremy heard a girl ask her friend as they filed into the auditorium.

"No clue, but it has to be someone with major nerve," the other girl replied loudly. "I'm just glad we finally got those jerks from MacArthur!"

Jeremy smiled despite his intention to keep cool. Funny how people liked to take pride in things they had nothing to do with.

But his flush of pleasure at being a school celebrity—albeit an invisible one—turned to ice when he saw the expression on Powell's face as she strode to the podium. She looked decidedly different than she had the morning of the gnomes, and Jeremy wondered if there was any way she could find out who had decorated the bus.

That was what he wanted, he reminded himself. To be unmasked as the person behind the pranks. But maybe not in front of the whole school . . .

"Girls," Powell said once they were all settled. In spite of his nerves, Jeremy made a little grumbling noise. "Now, I know I said some things about merry pranksters, and that sometimes pranks can be fun, but as some of you saw last night, not everyone agrees. I fear some of you took my words as permission to continue with these shenanigans and for that I am truly sorry. This is my fault."

Claudia, sitting next to Jeremy, made a face.

"But, even so," Powell continued. "I really must stress that this kind of behavior is not going to be tolerated any-more. I'll let it go this one time, because I feel like I wasn't clear enough previously. But let me be as frank as possible now: If there are any more pranks, I will find out who is doing them, and that person, or people, will be severely punished."

The girls sat dumbly as Powell waited for the message to sink in.

Claudia was extremely pleased with herself after the assem-bly. "See? I told you," she said. "If there's another prank, you'll be severely punished. So now we only have to do one more! You'll be kicked out before Christmas."

Jeremy smiled weakly at her. Something about the way Powell had put such emphasis on the words "severely punished" had his insides quaking. But he had to keep his eye on the final goal.

Besides, now that he knew he was just one step away from getting expelled, it was finally time to stop being terrified of talking to his costar.

It was stupid, honestly. Ever since auditions he'd been tongue-tied and mute around Anna, except when they were saying their lines. How could he go to a new school, and be a whole new person, if he couldn't even talk to a girl he thought was interesting? Especially when they were spending almost every afternoon working on a movie together.

Besides, he wasn't the same old Jeremy Miner anymore. He was the kind of kid who pulled a massive prank on his school's archrival. Talking to one girl couldn't be scarier than that, could it?

His plan was to talk to her during rehearsals on Friday, so if she laughed in his face he'd have the weekend to recover. Or change his name and run away to another country, depending on how humiliating it was.

⇨

But, on Friday, Claudia threw him for a loop when they met in the band room to set up for that day's shooting.

"Sooooooo," she said, drawing out the word in her most exaggerated way. The two of them were moving chairs to clear space for the sets that were folded and stuck in a corner. "I heard a little rumor your mom went out to lunch with Reynolds."

"Ha, ha. Very funny," Jeremy said, shoving a few more chairs toward the window. "My mom never goes out to lunch; she always brings something from home."

"Well," Claudia said, still in that annoying voice, "maybe she changed her mind this time."

"Or it could have been a work thing," he persevered. "They're both on that Legacy Committee together."

"Maybe," she said, with a strange smile. "Or maybe it was, like, a date."

"You can't be serious." The very idea was ludicrous. But something about the way Claudia was looking at him made him feel like she was telling the truth, at least as far as she knew. "With Reynolds? But he's married."

"Not anymore. Don't you remember that Film Club meeting two years ago where he wasn't wearing his wedding ring and Delaney suggested epic love stories as a movie theme? He said love was an illusion, the sooner we figured that out the better, and he went on and on and we were like, oh my God, this is so awkward, when is he going to stop, and it was totally horrible?"

Jeremy shook his head.

"Figures. You're a guy. You never remember anything, like, important. Anyway, he's divorced; she's divorced. What's the harm?"

"What's the harm? Are you kidding me? He's one of my teachers!" Jeremy said. "That's got to be illegal or something."

"I don't think it is," Claudia said. "Besides, maybe he'll give you an A now."

"But that would be like . . ." He couldn't even finish the sentence. He hoped Claudia was joking around. Or if it was true, and they had gone out, it was only to discuss something for work or because his mother had forgotten her lunch or some other innocent reason. "Besides, I'm already getting an A."

"Then what do you have to worry about?"

"What do I have to worry about? It's gross!"

The door opened, and a few extras came in, so he

ignored Claudia's provocative smile and tried to concentrate on stacking the chairs up against the wall just so. He needed to stay focused.

Jeremy's mother had started dating a couple of years earlier. She was still kind of attractive, Jeremy thought, for a mom. And pretty young. So it made sense guys would ask her out and she would go.

When Jeremy and his sisters were little, she hadn't wanted them to meet her dates. She would leave them with a babysitter and go off by herself on mysterious outings they would speculate about for hours.

But now that Jeremy and his sisters were older, they knew a lot more about her dating life, and they realized it was anything but mysterious. She didn't even call the men she dated boyfriends. She used duller words, like "companion" and "friend." For a while she had been taking a wine-tasting class with a professor named Gary. And every couple of weeks she had dinner or saw a movie with Unintentionally Creepy Phil. Less frequently she would go to a gallery in North Adams with Mr. Blah. Jeremy couldn't bother to remember his real name. He didn't know how his mother could stand any of them.

And her dates just made him miss his father, imperfect as he was, and what it had been like when it was the five of them together.

He sat quietly as the first scene got under way, trying not to look at Reynolds, who had arrived late, as usual, and was huddled in the corner with his newspaper. Was he smiling more today? What was that all about?

A girl named Carrie argued with Claudia about her part. "I don't see why my character has to die the minute we get off the ship," she said. "It's not fair."

"But you're the first person off the ship," Claudia said, as though that explained everything.

"But that doesn't mean I have to die," the girl protested.

"Of course it does!" Claudia said. She paused, took a deep breath, and, like she was explaining the alphabet to a two-year-old, said, "You're the first person off the ship and you're not a lead character. You have to die to make the audience realize how dangerous this place is for the characters they actually care about! It's like a science-fiction law."

"Well, maybe I could be gravely wounded and then come back at the end and save the day?"

Claudia looked down at the floor and then up at the lights with her hands in the air as if imploring the heavens for assistance.

"You. Don't. Even. Have. A. Name," she said. "You. Are. Space. Ensign. Number. Four."

"I was thinking about that, actually, and I think my character's name should be Francine," the girl said.

"You don't have a name!" Claudia almost shouted. "Space ensigns without names don't save the day!"

Claudia's tantrum created a good opportunity for Jeremy to take a seat next to Anna, who was sitting on a plastic chair with her face buried in a textbook.

"Having fun?" he asked in what he hoped was a calm, jovial tone. He had planned on sounding bored and cool, like Claudia's brother, Ian, but instead his voice came out sounding sort of . . . squeaky.

Anna looked up at Claudia, who was slamming scenery around, and then down at her math book. She gave Jeremy a quizzical look, but all she said was, "Um . . ."

"I mean making the movie," he added quickly.

"Oh yeah," she said. "Yeah, it's cool."

She looked down at her book again.

"So you just moved here, right?" He couldn't let the conversation lapse now that he'd finally mustered the courage to talk to her.

"Yeah, a couple of weeks ago," she said. "My mom got remarried and we moved up here from Connecticut, and I needed to go someplace for school and she's an alumna so . . ." She trailed off.

"Well, St. Edith's is a great school," Jeremy said, feeling compelled to defend it. "There are lots of clubs. None of the other schools around here have a Film Club like this one."

"Oh," Anna said. She looked like she wanted to go back to her book.

"But it's not just Film Club," Jeremy said wildly. "I know you probably think I just do Film Club and that I'm the only guy, you know, in the Film Club, but that's not all I do, not even half of it. There are tons of other things. *Tons.*"

Anna nodded, but her eyes shifted to the side.

"You know what? We should run lines sometime, you and me. We could get together and practice without all this, um, distracting stuff," he plowed on. "Maybe Saturday?"

"Oh, I can't on Saturday," she said. "I have ice skating lessons."

"You skate?" he asked. "That's really great. I do too . . . not figure skating, of course, hockey. The hockey team."

This was total fiction. Jeremy skated once a year when his mom got it into her head that they should have a family outing, and he usually only lasted about a half hour. Weak ankles.

"St. Edith's has a hockey team?"

"Oh, no, not St. Edith's. The one in town. The Red Mill Rangers." He'd completely made that up, but it sounded like something real. "We were state champs," he lied. He felt like he was digging a big hole for himself. The minute she saw him on ice skates she would know he was faking. "Until I busted my knee," he said sadly. "And now the doctors say I'll never skate again."

Was it too much? But she looked genuinely sympathetic. "Oh, I'm sorry. That stinks."

"It's okay," he said, gazing off into the distance as though at the retreating back of his NHL dreams. "Now I do stuff like Film Club."

"Oh." Again she turned back to her book.

"And I'm in a band!" He couldn't help himself. He felt like if he could just say something to impress her she would look up—really look up—and see him, the real Jeremy. Or maybe not the real Jeremy, but the cooler, more interesting version of himself that existed in the fake conversations he had with her in his head.

A loud snort came from the windowsill behind them. Jeremy jerked back to look and saw Emily curled up on the ledge, smirking, with her camera cradled on her lap. He hadn't even realized she was there.

He glared at her. Anna didn't seem to notice, though, and looked at her math book again.

"I guess I'll let you do your homework," he said, as though he was being gallant and she wasn't already focused on something else. He slid back down the row of seats to the very opposite end, by a drum set, closed his eyes, and wondered how much it would hurt to put his head between two cymbals and slam them together.

He sensed someone next to him and looked up quickly, hoping against hope it was Anna.

But it was only Emily.

"A band, huh?" she said, in a teasing sort of voice. "I had no idea you were in a *band*."

"Just forget it, Emily," he whispered hoarsely. He didn't

want Anna to hear. But the room was as noisy as ever. Claudia had wheeled in one of the school's beat-up TVs so she could play a PBS documentary on howler monkeys in order to give the background players inspiration for the interscene screeching she wanted them to do. The somber tones of the announcer combined with the high-pitched yelping from both the TV and the newly invigorated extras made it unlikely anyone could hear Emily unless she was screaming. But that didn't stop him from wishing she would go away.

"And a hockey team?" Emily asked. "You were on a championship hockey team? Amazing. Until your tragic knee accident, of course."

"Drop it, okay? I have to do my homework, and it's hard enough without you babbling at me."

Across from where they were sitting, the Greek chorus of alien monkeys prepared for the next scene by putting on their antennae and claws. Two of the girls squabbled over whose eyeball stalks were supposed to be red and who had the lavender.

Girls were weird. It never ceased to amaze Jeremy how

they would eagerly dress up in any crazy getup if you said they were being an alien, but God forbid you asked them to play a part written for a boy.

The whole room was a madhouse, and no matter how many times Claudia screamed "Quiet on the set!" the noise only grew.

"Does anyone know how to walk on their hands? Anyone?" Claudia hollered at a group of extras. The actors looked at their shoes.

"Sorry. I thought that it was rather unusual that you were boldly lying to that girl," Emily said. She was attempting to sound sarcastic, but instead it came out impossibly prim. "It was just, you know, interesting to me."

"We were just talking," Jeremy said. "And you shouldn't have been listening in on someone else's conversation anyway."

"Fine," she said. "It's not like I care or anything."

She sounded genuinely hurt, which softened his glare. He may have been the world's biggest loser, but there was no reason to take it out on Emily. "What are you up to today, anyway?"

"Oh, taking some pictures," she said, holding up the camera. "I told Claudia I'd make a program for the movie screening."

"Are you sure that's a good idea?" Jeremy remembered Claudia's reaction to Emily's audition posters. He could only imagine what a program would inspire.

"Oh, don't worry; she's already given me a list of all the things I can't do," Emily said with an uncharacteristic eye roll. "But I'll come up with something cool, once I get pictures of everybody in the cast and crew. Actually"—and here she stood up—"I better get started."

She paused for a moment, like she was waiting for him to say something. Then she walked off.

# FIFTEEN

**THAT NIGHT AT HOME JEREMY WONDERED IF**
there was some way he could figure out where Anna took
skating lessons. Probably at the big rink in town. Number thirteen, Justin Stedman, had a skating birthday party
there once. He could show up and act like he hung out
there all the time. Maybe he could find that old brace
Rachel had used when she'd broken her wrist and put it
on his knee. But what would he say when he saw Anna?
How could he explain being there without sounding like a
complete idiot? It was hopeless.

He was supposed to go to Claudia's later to watch a
movie with some of the Film Club people. Normally his
mom would drive him—even though she acted grumpy
about driving him places, she also worried he would get hit
by a car biking at night. But it turned out she had a dinner
date, and she was so completely distracted she gave him
permission to go into Red Mill without even asking how
he was going to get there.

"And could you empty the dishwasher?" she asked. "I haven't had a chance to do it yet."

"Okay?" he said, as though the request was an odd one. When it came to chores, he tried to strike a tone that made him sound like he really didn't understand the question. He had discovered recently that acting helpless and asking a lot of questions when his mother told him to do something was a good way to get out of it.

He didn't know why this worked. It definitely annoyed her. But eventually she would just take over and do it herself. He'd noticed this acquired helplessness incited the same reaction in other women he knew, like Emily when they were doing homework together or Claudia when she wanted him to move lights around or plug in sound equipment for the Film Club. It was like he'd cracked some sort of code, a way to annoy girls but also get them to leave you alone. Sometimes he wondered if this was the sort of thing he would have learned sooner if his dad had been around.

This time, though, his mother didn't seem to notice his tone. She just said, "Good."

"Who are you going out with tonight, anyway?" he asked. "Phil?"

Her expression was so unusual it forced him to ask for details, against his will.

"No," she said. "Somebody new. Somebody . . . different." And she flashed him an almost saucy smile as she walked out of the kitchen.

He remembered Claudia saying his mother had gone out to lunch with Reynolds, and he seriously hoped his language arts teacher wasn't the reason his mother was smiling like that.

Shortly before six the doorbell rang. Jeremy was sitting in the living room, flipping channels. His mother was in her bedroom, and his sisters were nowhere he could see, so he muted the TV and got up to answer the door.

It was Mr. Reynolds. He was wearing the same kind of beige sport coat he always had on, but no tie, and instead of a plain white or blue shirt he wore a plaid one. He was also smiling in a way he never seemed to smile in class.

"Hi, Jeremy," he said warmly. "It's nice to see you. Is your mom ready?"

He'd had this conversation before, only with Mr. Blah and Unintentionally Creepy Phil and that other guy, the one she'd only went out with once, who had the fake tan and drove a Hummer. It was the kind of thing men asked when they rang the doorbell because they were there to pick up his mother for a . . . date.

He had so fervently hoped Claudia was lying. Inside his head he heard the crash of worlds colliding.

"Um, no," he said. Reynolds's smile faltered, and Jeremy felt the urge to stand up a little straighter. "Um, please come in."

Reynolds didn't say anything about the ums, like he would have at school, just kept the smile plastered on his face as Jeremy led him into the living room. "You have a lovely home," he said, as though the living room wasn't a jumble of magazines and schoolbooks and other junk, and as if Jeremy had anything to do with the decor.

The seconds ticked by. Jeremy wondered if he should say something, but what? He considered going to his room and leaving Reynolds by himself, but that seemed wrong too.

It felt like an eternity later—but really it was probably only two minutes—when Jeremy's mother appeared. She was wearing a dress, a blue one he'd never seen before that sort of wrapped around her front and clung to her hips.

Jeremy's mother never wore a dress on dates. The last time he'd seen her in a dress was probably Great Aunt Mary's funeral two years ago.

"Hi, Bob," she said with a wide smile. "Sorry to keep you waiting. Thanks for letting him in, Jeremy." She smiled at Jeremy, too, almost as though she expected him to say something, but he felt like he was in a movie where he didn't know his lines, or one of those *Twilight Zone* episodes Emily always wanted to watch on New Year's.

So he stood, dumbfounded, as his mom came over in her new dress, and they bustled around him, Reynolds refusing an offer of water, Mom getting her coat and then giving instructions—"Listen to Rachel, be back by ten, don't stay up too late"—and left Jeremy in the middle of the living room. It was as if he were expected to act like all of this was the most normal thing in the world.

The noise of the car pulling out of the driveway woke him from the spell. It was too early to go to Claudia's, but he needed a distraction.

"I'm going to Emily's," he shouted upstairs. Rachel shouted something noncommittal, which he took as a yes. So he grabbed his coat from the closet and trudged across the yard, leaving black footprints in the white early winter frost.

Emily was in her den, leafing through one of those Japanese comic books where all the characters had eyes the size of dessert plates and watching some lame Disney Channel show.

"Hi," she said. "I didn't know you were coming over." She sounded stiff, like she was angry but trying not to show it.

"Sorry," he said, though he didn't know why. He'd always come over like this before, without calling or setting up plans. That was just the way things were between him and Emily. But there was something formal and odd in the way she sat there not looking at him.

"I thought you'd be hanging out with that girl from the movie, Anna?" Emily said, still flipping through her comic book.

"Why would you even think that?" he asked, though he could feel a blush rising.

"Or maybe your band has a gig," she said. "What is it you play again? The imaginary bass?"

"Come on, Emily, I was kidding around."

"Well, sit down," she said, but she waved at the armchair, not at the sofa where she was sitting. He sat. "I'm sure you only came over here because you want something," she said, still in that stiff voice. "So what's up?"

"Oh, nothing," he said. "Well, except my mom went on a date tonight."

"Oh?" Emily said. "That's nice." And her eyes went back to the TV.

Jeremy watched her face. "With Reynolds."

That made her look up at him. "Really? No way."

"Yeah," he said. "Apparently they've been, like, talking at work and having lunch and stuff, and now they're going out on an actual date."

"That must be so weird," Emily said. "But I like Mr. Reynolds, don't you?"

"No!" Jeremy said, incredulous. "Of course not. He's so stuck-up and annoying."

Emily laughed. "That's because he's a teacher. He's a good guy, if you give him a chance. A couple of weeks ago, when I almost quit Film Club, he talked to me for a long time and it really helped."

"You almost quit Film Club?"

"Well, I think he's a lot better than those other guys your mom goes out with," Emily said, ignoring the question. "Like that creepy guy Phil—and the really dull one."

"Well, I'm not so sure."

"At least give him a chance," she said. "What if your mom starts dating him really seriously? What if they get married?"

"Oh God," Jeremy said, and whacked himself in the face with a burgundy throw pillow.

"Sorry, sorry!" Emily said, but she was laughing. Whatever iciness had been in her voice when he first showed up had melted, at least temporarily. "I'm sure it's nothing, just dinner."

"I sincerely hope you're right."

"Aren't I always right?" she teased. "Anyway, you want to watch a movie or something? Take your mind off things? I could make popcorn. I'll even watch *Star Wars*. . . ."

"Nah," Jeremy said, checking his watch. "I've got to get to Claudia's."

"Oh, right," she said. "Silly me. I thought you came over here to actually talk to me, not so your mom doesn't know what you're up to."

"That's not true!" he said, but he felt a wave of guilt as he flashed back to how he had done exactly that when he and Claudia went gnoming.

"Don't think I can't put two and two together, Jeremy," she said. "You and Claudia always whispering and plotting, and then all these pranks start happening? I'm not a moron. I bet you have that girl Anna in on it too."

"What?" he said, arranging his face into what he hoped was an incredulous expression. "I have no idea what you're talking about."

"Whatever," she said. "It's not like what I think matters to you anyway."

She was starting to freak him out. He knew she suspected something, but he hadn't really taken it seriously. He didn't want Emily to mess up the whole plan before they were ready.

He stood up. "Well, I gotta go. Thanks for listening to me vent."

"Any time," she said, but she didn't look at him, just stared at the television screen.

# SIXTEEN

**THE NEXT DAY JEREMY FOUND HIMSELF UNCHARI-**
tably irritated by the way his mother smiled as she mixed
waffle batter and put out containers of juice and milk. She
shouldn't have been smiling this early on a Saturday morning. Or making homemade waffles. She should have been
chugging coffee and grimly slamming things as usual.

He wasn't going to ask about it, though. He wouldn't
let her know she'd gone out with the worst possible person
for her to go out with in the entire universe and it was
killing him. He wasn't going to give her the satisfaction.

Then Jane came in.

"So, Mom, how was your date?" she asked, completely oblivious.

"Fine," their mom said. "Great, actually."

She gave Jane's hair an affectionate stroke. "Bob is so
funny; we had the best time. He told me this story—well,
I don't know if you kids would find it interesting." She
chuckled like she was remembering something. "But we
laughed so much."

"So," Jeremy said, "we're calling him Bob now?"

"*We're* not calling him Bob. *I'm* calling him Bob," she said. "Actually, I've always called him that, for your information."

"Just not, like, regularly around the house," Jeremy said. "So I guess I was confused."

"Do you have some sort of problem this morning, Jeremy?" his mother asked with a bemused expression.

"Just that you're dating his language arts teacher," Rachel said, sliding into the room and grabbing a cup of yogurt from the fridge. She gave Jeremy a sympathetic smile.

Their mother laughed again, a different laugh than Jeremy was used to. Younger sounding. It disturbed him.

"It was one date!" she said. "Really," she added, turning to Jeremy. "We're taking it one day at a time, getting to know each other."

"I thought you already knew each other from work," Jeremy said grumpily. "Calling him Bob and everything."

There was that laugh again. "This is different," she said. "A different kind of getting to know each other."

Jeremy made a gagging noise. He couldn't help it.

"Jeremy!" his mother said. Something like that should

have gotten him sent to his room at least. But she just laughed even more and went back to her waffle iron.

As if being the only boy at St. Edith's wasn't bad enough, now this.

"Oh God," he said, so low his mother couldn't hear him, and put his head down on the table.

By Monday morning he was seriously dreading going to Reynolds's class. What if he said something about the date?

It didn't help that the girls from the volleyball team laughed at him again as he passed the first floor bathroom. Did they know about his mom and Reynolds? Is that why they were laughing?

Jeremy could only imagine how mortified he would be if the whole class found out his mother had gone out with their language arts teacher. What would they think? What would Anna think? He hoped with all his might that Reynolds hadn't had as good a time as Jeremy's mom apparently did.

But Reynolds was exactly the same. Maybe a little more prone to smiling than usual. Jeremy couldn't tell, and he didn't want to think about what that might mean. Other than that, the class could have been any language arts class on any other day. Unnervingly so.

Even though it wasn't Thanksgiving yet, it snowed every day that week. Not enough for school to be canceled, just long, slow storms that left drifts everywhere and made anyone older than ten morose and cranky. Jeremy spent most afternoons filming scenes for the movie, which wasn't getting any better. In fact, he was convinced it was the worst movie ever made. He was also beginning to suspect that Claudia hadn't actually found this script in a bookstore but had written every last miserable word herself. He knew better than to voice that theory, though.

But nothing was as bad as the romantic scenes between him and Anna.

"Ever since you came into my life," Jeremy choked out, looking at the floor. It was a pivotal scene, where he was supposed to confess his feelings as the aliens began their attack. "I've—I've—I've . . . been . . . I've . . ."

"CUT!" Claudia yelled. "Come on, Jeremy, this is the sixth take!"

For some reason every single person in the cast and

crew seemed to be there watching as he stood in front of the teetering scenery and tried to tell Anna—well, technically Dr. Zizmor—that he was falling in love with her. It was brutal.

But he plowed ahead. "Come away with me," he said without looking at her. He reached out to grab her arm and to his horror, hit her in the neck.

"Oof," Anna said, stumbling backward in surprise. The crowd of girls giggled, then—as she bumped into the scenery and it came tumbling down on top of her and Jeremy—roared.

"That's it!" Claudia yelled. Her voice was hoarse from screaming. "I'm cutting this scene. I can't bear to watch this train wreck one more time."

Jeremy burned red. He didn't know if he was more embarrassed at the scene or the fact that he'd botched it so badly.

In the end Claudia cut most of the romantic parts so they could get to work on other, more important scenes, like the one where the space dirigible blew up, and a pivotal one where Jeremy, as Captain Flynn, got caught in the Evil Space Monkey King's agony beam.

Meanwhile, on Wednesday night his mother went out with Mr. Reynolds to see a jazz band—and she had never in her dating history gone out during the week. Or, come to think of it, gone to a bar to see a band play. Sure, she told stories about following some band around one summer in college, but that was so long ago it was like she was talking about a fictional character.

And she was supposed to go out with him again that coming weekend. Jeremy couldn't remember the last time she went out with someone two weekends in a row. Usually weeks went by between dates, like she thought going on them was something she ought to do because it was good for her rather than actual fun. Sort of the way most people feel about flossing.

"Three dates in a week," Jeremy said to Claudia as they got drinks from the cafeteria during a break in filming that Friday. "Who does that?"

"People who really like each other," Claudia said, sipping her iced tea thoughtfully.

"Oh great."

"Come on. Don't you want your mother to be happy?"

"Yeah, but not with him," he said.

"Well, I don't think you get to choose."

"I know," he said, pretending to bang his head against the side of the vending machine. "Shoot me now, please."

"Not until after the movie is finished," she said. "And if you get kicked out, Reynolds won't be your teacher anymore, right? So that would be a bonus. No more being the last boy, no more Reynolds in language arts, no more St. Edith's."

"Which is why," he said, with more confidence than he felt, "we need to come up with another prank. But this time, it's my turn."

If there was any benefit to his mother's newly invigorated social life it was that he was suddenly far freer to leave the house, because she was never there. All he had to do was tell Rachel he was going to Emily's. She never asked questions, like his mother would.

So the following week when his mother was out again—they were going to a movie, she said, and dinner and would be back late—he said good-bye to his sisters and walked around the block to where Claudia was waiting in a pickup truck her brother had borrowed from a friend, just like they'd planned. In the back he could see a couple of plastic snow shovels, and he added the one he'd taken from his garage to the stack.

It was the first prank Jeremy had come up with all on his own. Claudia was skeptical, but he knew it was going to be the best one yet. He'd worked out every detail like a criminal mastermind, down to the piece of paper in his pocket with preliminary calculations of how much snow they could carry in a full-size pickup truck.

Jeremy instructed Ian to drive past St. Edith's to a secluded park about three blocks away from school, behind the old train station, which was being renovated into a café. The place was deserted in the cold and blanketed in a deep layer of snow.

"I think we should get the snow here, so they can't figure out where it came from," Jeremy said. He liked being in charge for once and deliberately made his voice as deep as possible. "That will heighten the . . . impact."

"Whatever you say; you're the boss," Claudia said. Steam came out of her mouth as she talked. She looked like a teapot.

When he was little, Jeremy had loved the way cold air

made him breathe steam. Sometimes he'd pretend he was smoking an invisible pipe. But now it just meant "cold," and as excited as he was, he wished he'd put on long johns or something under his jeans.

The sky was swirled with gray like the shale they'd studied on their last school hiking trip, and the snow was crusted over, sparkling in the dim light. Unfortunately, that just made it heavy and hard to shovel. And while Ian had driven them there, that was the extent of his involvement. He stayed in the cab of the borrowed truck, listening to music and looking annoyingly warm.

They didn't talk, just worked. Jeremy lifted shovelful after shovelful into the back of the truck until it was overflowing—which took ages—until Claudia stopped, leaned on her own shovel, and said, "I think that's probably enough, don't you?"

Jeremy consulted the paper in his pocket. If his calculations were correct, they should have at least a ton of snow in there, possibly more. That had to be plenty, right? "I think so," he said with more confidence than he felt.

He could feel blisters forming inside his mittens, which

were coated in slicks of refrozen snow that made holding the shovel difficult. He'd made the mistake of wearing his itchiest pair, the baby-blue-and-yellow ones his mother had knitted last Christmas to match his St. Edith's uniform.

He tossed his shovel on top of the snow mound and climbed gratefully into the cab, where the heater was blasting.

"I think we should park the truck in Elmer's usual spot," Claudia said. "Anyone who sees it will just think it's his, and it's right by the fire escape."

"Perfect," Jeremy said, wishing he'd thought of that idea himself. It was supposed to be his prank, after all.

Once Ian stopped the truck, Claudia stood on the back and hopped onto the bottom of the fire escape ladder. Jeremy handed her the bucket tied with rope. She nimbly climbed to the roof, two stories up, and then looped the rope around the top of the fire escape to make a pulley. She lowered it down, and Jeremy filled it with snow. Ian continued to sit in the warmth of the car, ignoring them until Jeremy gave him Claudia's video camera and asked him to take footage of the pulley system he had designed, since it was key to making the prank work. "For posterity," he said with a smile.

Claudia continued to dump bucketfuls of snow onto the roof, until Jeremy had sent up most of it. Then he joined her.

He was tired from all the shoveling, but it felt glorious to be on top of the school at night. He could see the stars above and the streetlights glittering on the snow below. Claudia had tossed the snow into a big, loose pile. It seemed like even more now that it was out of the truck.

"Wouldn't it be cool if we built one of those snow sculptures? The kind they show on TV?" she asked.

"There's no way we could do that," Jeremy said a little impatiently. "We should just stick to the plan and make the biggest snowman we can."

Together they rolled the truckload of snow into enormous balls and set up their creation right at the very edge of the flat roof, over the majestic school entryway, where everyone would see it the minute they approached the building. When they were done, Jeremy produced a couple of charcoal briquettes and a carrot from his pockets to make the face and buttons. Claudia pulled out a pipe and stuck it in what would be the snowman's mouth.

"Where'd you get a pipe?" Jeremy asked in wonderment.

"I have my sources," she said with a smile.

Jeremy put two of his mother's wooden spoons into the sides of the snowman as arms.

But Claudia frowned and fiddled with them. "I wish we had something better, something bigger, like branches," she said. "I don't know if these will even show up."

Jeremy contemplated their creation. It was tall, taller than both of them. "How about this?" he suggested, stripping off his mittens and putting them on the spoon ends. It's not like he'd need mittens in St. Edith's colors at his new school. And maybe this could be his ultimate calling card, identifying him as the prankster. The mastermind behind it all.

The two of them stood there, looking at the massive snowman peering down at the front entrance to the school, and the twinkly winter stars, and the town spread out in the darkness. He couldn't see Claudia's face, but he knew she was smiling, because he was smiling.

"Epic," she said softly.

For a minute Jeremy forgot about how cold it was and

just felt thrilled and free. Or close enough to free. Tomorrow would be a tough day, he was sure, but he was prepared to face it.

Because despite all his doubts, he was finally doing something to change his lot in life. He was finally in charge of his own destiny. And it felt really, really good.

# SEVENTEEN

THE NEXT MORNING JEREMY GOT A RIDE TO school with his mother and sisters. He was nervous, since if all went well, by the end of the day he would be sent packing forever. That was a good thing; it was what would happen in between the drive to school and that triumphant moment of freedom that had his stomach in knots.

The weather had warmed up overnight, and a light rain began falling as soon as they got into the car. He just hoped the rain wouldn't ruin everything.

As they drove into Red Mill, he steeled himself for the scene he expected to greet him at the doors of St. Edith's. Something similar to the morning of the gnome invasion, probably. Girls standing around, teachers grumbling.

But what faced him this time was far different.

He knew something was up the moment his mother turned the corner next to St. Edith's. She abruptly came to a dead halt.

"What's this all about?" she asked no one in particular.

Cars were backed up in front of the school, and shouting

men milled about near a huge truck with flashing lights. The students who had managed to get out of buses or their parents' cars had been corralled in the teachers' parking lot, where they were now stamping their feet and whispering.

"Get out and see what's going on, Jeremy," his mother instructed. She didn't have to ask him twice.

He made his way down the sidewalk until a man in a bright orange vest stopped him. "Don't come any closer," the man warned.

"Why? What's going on?"

"We're keeping everyone out of the building until we can assess the damage."

"The . . . damage?"

"From the flooding," the man said, looking over his shoulder. "Somehow a ton of snow got on top of the roof." Here Jeremy winced, but the man wasn't looking at him. "Nobody knows how; it was shoveled after the last storm. Maybe one of those pranks. Anyway, the weight broke a hole in the roof, and all the water came down into the lobby and the computer lab in the basement. It's a mess. Gotta check for structural damage. These old buildings, you never know."

Jeremy gulped, but the man didn't notice, just turned back to the other workers. Jeremy knew he should return to the car and tell his mother what was going on, but he needed a moment to think about what to say.

So instead he wandered over to the parking lot and joined the throng of girls grousing about being stuck outside, even though it was warmer today than it had been all week. Their voices swirled around him.

"Did you hear Sabrina Driscoll went in the side door and ended up slipping and falling? She sprained her ankle."

"How can water do that much damage, though?" another girl asked. "Haven't there been floods before?"

"It's not just the water, dummy. I heard that it's not normal snow; it's snow that somebody put up there, with all the salt and ice melt and stuff mixed in. That stuff is horrible for floors; that's why my mom makes us take our boots off in the kitchen."

"I bet it was those MacArthur Prep idiots getting back at us for the bus thing. Somebody said it was supposed to be a snowman. A prank."

An eighth-grade girl Jeremy only knew by sight lowered her voice. "Well, I heard it was the volleyball team."

LEE GJERTSEN MALONE

Jeremy stiffened and bit his lip.

"What?" another girl said. "Why would they do something like this?"

"I don't know, but there's a rumor going around that they were talking in the bathroom about pulling something massive before their big tournament. I bet they did the bus too."

"How could they have done that? It was in the middle of a match."

"I don't know," the eighth grader replied. "Some of the people on the bench could have snuck out. They're going to get in huge trouble."

Jeremy hadn't considered the idea that someone else could be blamed for the pranks. And the volleyball team? That meant . . . Rachel.

The day only went downhill from there.

Eventually the teachers decided to let the kids use the rear entrance to get to the auditorium and their classrooms. Jeremy expected morning assembly to be full of Powell yelling, but she didn't even show up. Instead the dean of students offered a few notes and that was it. The students stepped carefully around the school, as though the building might collapse underneath them, but the main problems seemed to be in the front entryway, where the ancient oak floors had been warped by the snow, ice, and water that had fallen through the roof and then leaked into the basement. Thousands of dollars' worth of computer equipment was ruined, half the power was out, and all day workers banged and clanged around the front of the school, making noises that sounded far too much like sawing and ripping up wood.

But the worst part didn't happen until he got home. He walked, since he didn't have his bike and his mother wasn't in the office when he tried to find her; she'd gone home with Rachel, one of the other secretaries said.

And when he walked through the door, it was Rachel he heard sobbing in her room upstairs. Perfect Rachel who never cried and always kept it all together.

Jeremy's mom was sitting in the kitchen with a cup of tea. "Oh, there you are," she said vacantly, as though it was his fault she'd forgotten about him.

"What happened?" He almost didn't want to know.

"Your sister's been suspended from school for a week,"

she said in a voice he found hard to parse. "The whole team's been banned from playing. They'll be able to cheer on the JV team at the big tournament since the hotel's already booked, but not participate. "

"Oh no." He could feel the blood pulsing in his ears.

"And that's not the worst of it," she said with a deep sigh. "It's all going on her permanent record. She's never going to get a scholarship now, not after this."

Jeremy suddenly couldn't swallow. "How can that . . . I mean . . . why?"

His mother looked up at him. "You think schools want to pay to bring in troublemakers? Hah! No, the rich kids manage to talk their way in anywhere, but if you want a scholarship you've got to do everything right." She shook her head. "And she's worked so hard! I just don't understand why she would throw it all away for something this stupid."

She looked down at her tea again, and Jeremy walked out of the room. He took a deep breath and trudged up the stairs. He didn't know what he was going to say to Rachel. For an instant he felt flushed with anger—not at Powell or even himself, but at his dad, off on his boat, never there to teach Jeremy the things he was only beginning to realize he needed to know.

"Hey."

Rachel lay flat on her bed, the purple bedspread neat as always, staring at the ceiling. "I don't want to talk about it."

"That's okay." He wondered if he should leave, but that felt wrong.

She turned slightly. "All we were doing was talking about dyeing a stripe in our hair or wearing our uniforms backward one day," she said, her voice heavy and ragged with tears. "We didn't do any of this. But Powell won't even listen. She says they found a mitten of mine at the so called scene of the crime." She buried her head in her pillow.

The mitten. His mitten. Rachel had the same kind, the ones their mother had made last Christmas. But it wasn't her mitten. He felt like he needed to say something, but the lump in his throat was too big. All he could muster was "I'm sorry."

She hugged herself. "I don't know what I'm going to do now. I really don't."

He didn't know what to think. Rachel was always the perfect one. The one who acted more like a grown-up than their mom sometimes. It usually drove him crazy, but seeing her like this, he would have given anything for her to be standing the way she normally did, her school shirt crisp and perfect, every hair in place—the family star. Not lying on her bed, a mess.

Especially when it was his fault. And he wanted to say that; he really did. To tell her that he could fix everything.

But the confession stayed deep inside him, like a ball of bile in his stomach.

Because he'd made a major mistake. The worst kind of mistake. Not just because he'd gotten his sister involved in all of this—which he was horribly sorry about—but also because he hadn't realized how big a problem getting in trouble would create. No scholarship to high school for Rachel definitely meant no scholarship for him if they found out what he'd done. Not to MacArthur Prep, not anywhere.

He had the sudden and very unsettling fear that his mother may have been right all along.

If he confessed to the pranks, there was no way he could go anywhere but the horribly bad local public school, where boys like him got beaten up every day and barely anybody graduated, at least according to his mother.

For the longest time that was exactly what he wanted: to get caught and expelled. But after what had happened with Rachel, suddenly the idea of actually being kicked out of school was scary, not exciting. He'd been so caught up in the thrill of the pranks, but he was beginning to suspect he should have thought this plan through. Because it wouldn't be just for eighth grade, but forever.

But if he didn't get kicked out, Rachel would.

# EIGHTEEN

**A HALF HOUR LATER JEREMY WAS SITTING IN** Mickey's with Claudia. He'd sent her a text and then rode furiously on his bike, trying not to panic. Claudia always knew what to do, he told himself. Claudia would have an answer.

But once he'd filled her in, they just sat, looking dejectedly at everything but each other.

"I'm really sorry," Claudia said. "Rachel's annoying, but she doesn't deserve this."

Jeremy just shook his head.

"Though I wonder . . . ," Claudia began, putting her chin in her hand.

"No, Claudia," Jeremy said sharply. "No more of your big ideas, okay?"

"Well, don't blame me; you came up with that snowman prank," she said. "And I'm not the one who was trying to get kicked out of school! I thought I was helping you."

"I know, I know," he said. "But I'm beginning to think

this was all a really bad idea. The pranks, getting kicked out of school, all of it."

"You're just upset about the volleyball team," Claudia said. "But at least they get to go to the tournament next weekend, right?"

"As spectators, though," Jeremy said. "And they were probably going to win the whole thing. I don't see how that's any kind of treat."

"Well, what if you do something while they're away?" Whitey said suddenly.

Jeremy jerked around. He hadn't even noticed him hovering near their table, fiddling with a bunch of salt and pepper shakers. Again, Jeremy couldn't tell if he worked at the restaurant or just liked to play around with random objects. But clearly Whitey had been eavesdropping.

"Like what?" Claudia said.

"Like one final prank on the whole school," Whitey said. "Bigger than all the rest. And then you"—he waved at Jeremy—"don't have to confess and get kicked out, but your sister's record will be cleared, since it obviously couldn't be her. And then it'll be done."

"Done," Jeremy repeated. Maybe that's what he wanted—for all of it to be simply finished.

"Have a seat," Claudia said to Whitey with a smile.

It turned out that Whitey had been eavesdropping, and not just today. He knew everything they'd been up to all semester. And he also knew a lot about pranks—more than both Jeremy and Claudia combined. His older brother had pulled some major ones before he "left" (Jeremy suspected he'd been kicked out of) the local high school, and while some were a little complicated, the thought process behind them was intriguing. Claudia and Jeremy's pranks were small potatoes compared to the ones Whitey knew about.

"So, I was thinking—what kind of doorknobs do they have at this fancy school of yours?" Whitey asked.

"Doorknobs?" Jeremy asked.

"Round, turny thing, helps you open the door. Try to keep up, Jeremy," the boy said, and Claudia snorted. "I bet they're the same ones they have at my school. They're putting them in everywhere around here. They have a lock on them, right?"

Jeremy nodded, though he wasn't really sure. But Claudia had a glint in her eye. "Yeah, they do. On the inside, so the teachers can lock us in if there's some kind of maniac in the halls. They put them in a few years ago as a safety thing."

"Exactly," Whitey said. "And they have a little switch? If you turn it, the door will lock on its own?"

"Yeah, yeah," Claudia said. "I think I know where you're going with this—but how do we pull it off?"

Jeremy was starting to get annoyed. "Could you guys please explain what you're talking about?" he asked, no longer caring if they accused him of not keeping up.

"Sorry," Whitey said. "What you've got to do is turn the doorknobs around, see? Take them off and switch them—during the night or something."

Claudia jumped in. "We'd have to leave the classroom doors open after, in the morning—sometimes the cleaning people do that, to keep track of what rooms they've cleaned. So nobody would think it was weird."

"The teachers come in and leave the doors open for the kids," Whitey continued. "But when it's time to start the class—"

"They close the doors and everyone is locked in!" Claudia finished. "And they might not even realize until the bell rings and they can't get out! It's brilliant."

"It's insane," Jeremy said. "There's no way that would work. How are we going to get into the school to switch all those doorknobs? It'll take hours."

"Your mom's keys," Claudia said. "You could take them."

"You want me to steal my mom's keys to the school? Are you insane?"

"It'll be fine," Claudia said. "Nobody's going to blame her. And if it happens on Monday, it'll be obvious to everyone that it couldn't possibly be Rachel and her friends. They'll be in Vermont the whole weekend. They're not coming back until Tuesday afternoon."

"But they still could have done the other pranks," Jeremy protested. "This wouldn't prove anything."

She gave him a classic Claudia side-eye. "You know Powell doesn't really believe it's her beloved championship volleyball team. She's just grasping at straws, trying to find the real culprit. She'll jump at the chance to blame someone else, trust me."

Jeremy could see the benefit of that. If there was evidence that someone else was behind the pranks, maybe Powell would change her mind. But he had another objection. "What about us? We're going to be in class too, locked in."

"So what?" Claudia said. "It'll be fun, and that'll make who did it all the more mysterious. Then, like he said"—she waved at Whitey—"it'll be done. For good."

Jeremy wasn't sure. The plan had a lot of potential problems, more than he could even articulate. But Whitey and Claudia seemed so sure it would work. Plus, it was a plan that meant neither he nor Rachel would get in trouble. And everything could go back the way it was. That was beginning to sound better and better to him.

He had a sudden thought about the bathroom, the one on the first floor. The way the girls disappeared through the door, with their mocking eyes, laughter echoing off the tile walls. It might be funny to lock that room at least, so some of those girls would be trapped and late for class. They wouldn't be laughing then.

They could even start a rumor that it was him—not a confession, just a rumor—and people would think he was cool and exciting. People like Anna.

"What's your name, anyway?" Claudia asked the boy when they had finished up the plans for the prank—it came together quickly, with Whitey providing all the logistics.

"Dylan," he said. "Dylan White. But most people call me Whitey, 'cause of my last name and because I'm so pale."

Claudia began to choke and waved at Jeremy, who had to thump her on the back until she could breathe.

"Sorry, soda went down the wrong pipe," she said to the boy, who looked confused. "I think I want to call you just Dylan, though, if that's okay. I'm not really into nicknames," she said, looking at him steadily, as though it wasn't a bald-faced lie. "Oh, and thanks for all your help. You're a lifesaver."

"Yeah, thanks," Jeremy said.

"No problem," Whitey—Dylan—said, and smiled for the first time. Jeremy noticed that unlike his white skin and his white hair, his teeth were almost gray. "You guys come in here all the time, and you're always talking about this stuff. It's cool I finally get to help. It'll be fun."

"Epic, even," Jeremy said with a pointed look at Claudia. And she smiled her widest smile.

# NINETEEN

JEREMY HAD BEEN FINE WITH WHITEY'S CONTRI-
bution to the prank-planning process—he had to admit
the kid knew way more about this kind of mischief than he
or Claudia did—but he was less than thrilled the following
Sunday afternoon as they were walking to meet him at
St. Edith's.

"Does he really have to come? He helped out with the
plan—that's fine—but do we have to actually bring him
with us?"

"Of course he has to come! It was his idea," Claudia said.

Jeremy sighed. They walked into the St. Edith's parking lot, where Whitey stood by himself in the dim late-
afternoon light. Whatever Claudia said, Jeremy refused to
call him Dylan.

"I wonder why he's always hanging around Mickey's,
though?" he whispered to Claudia. "Does he live there?"

"Of course not," she said. "I think he lives across the
street." She meant the trailer park. "Anyway, shut up," she

added, because Whitey had spotted them and was walking over with a wide smile on his face.

"Ready?" Whitey asked them.

"As ready as we'll ever be," Claudia replied with a smile.

Despite Jeremy's worries, the plot went off with only a limited and manageable amount of problems. Taking his mom's keys hadn't been hard. She'd left them lying in a jumble by her purse on the hall table, as usual.

And one of the benefits of this prank was that they didn't have to do it in the middle of the night. Nobody was at the school on a Sunday—the cleaning crew that supplemented Elmer's weekday efforts came on Saturday—so the place would be completely deserted until Monday morning.

Jeremy knew his mother had a key to the side door nearest the main office, so after a certain amount of trial and error—interrupted when they had to hide from passing cars—they figured out which key it was and then went inside.

Whitey had asked about security cameras and metal detectors and guards, which made Claudia laugh. "Are you kidding? This place is like Swiss cheese. If it was summer we wouldn't even have to use keys, we could just climb through an open window."

Whitey marveled at the wide hallways and arching windows. "This place is even nicer than it looks from the outside."

"Just don't check out the lobby," Claudia said with a snort. Jeremy stomped on her foot.

They went into one of the classrooms, where Whitey showed them how to unscrew, swap, and rescrew the doorknob, and then how to flip the switch so it would automatically lock. Then they each took one of the screwdrivers Whitey had brought and went off on their own to cover as much ground as possible.

Jeremy made a beeline for the bathroom on the first floor, the one where those girls who laughed at him every morning spent the last minutes before class primping. He smiled imagining all the confusion and yelling once they realized they were locked in.

It was mysterious, walking through the empty school in the darkness, and he had to stop himself from humming the James Bond theme music. Only the dim glow of the lights over the emergency exit doors showed the way.

Whitey had brought a couple of flashlights—he'd thought of everything—but he warned them to use them as little as possible so they wouldn't be spotted from outside.

When Jeremy walked past the dim lobby, its doors crisscrossed by yellow warning tape, he stopped and peered inside. Even in the darkness he could see how bad it was, with floorboards pulled up and tools and sawhorses everywhere. They were already repairing it thanks to emergency alumni donations, but he still cringed at the damage he'd caused. And not just to the building. Still, the whole point of this new prank was to try to repair what he could. And then, as Claudia had said, it would all be over.

He considered finding Anna's locker. Maybe he could slip a note inside, something cute and funny. People at normal schools did that, right? He felt that surge of self-confidence that always came with pulling pranks and almost convinced himself he could actually write something to her. But the lockers were on the other side of the building, and he had a limited amount of time, so he focused on the task at hand: the bathroom doorknob. Unscrew it, swap it, screw it back, flip the lock, and then open the door and leave it that way. He left with a satisfied smile.

The whole process took about an hour since they only did the classrooms used during first period. And the one bathroom. When they were finished, they met up by the side door, which Jeremy carefully locked with his mother's key.

"So, do you guys want to go to Mickey's and get a soda or something?" Whitey asked as they walked away from the school. "It's right by my house."

"Sure," Claudia said at the same time Jeremy said, "I can't. I have to get these keys back."

"Oh, right, that's cool," Whitey said, sounding as though he was trying to seem like he didn't care. Which isn't the same as actually not caring.

Whitey was a good kid, though, and he'd really helped them out. "Maybe we can meet up tomorrow, or the day after?" Jeremy said. "We'll tell you how it went."

"Yeah," Claudia said with relish. "This is going to be the boldest prank yet."

"And the last one," Jeremy reminded her.

"Of course."

The next day at morning assembly Jeremy could barely contain his mounting excitement. He was all nerves—

fingers drumming, toes tapping—until Claudia told him to quit it. He could tell she was nervous too, though, because she was chewing on the ends of her hair.

Powell droned on about "initiatives," but he barely cared. Instead he was waiting to see what would happen and trying not to act suspicious.

He smirked to himself when they got to first period language arts class and filed in through the open door. Reynolds closed it firmly behind them, and Jeremy could have sworn he heard the lock click.

Reynolds and the rest of the class opened books and began a discussion. Jeremy tried to focus on the page in front of him, but he kept imagining what would happen when the bell rang. Who would get up first and try the door? What would Reynolds do? When would they figure out they were locked in? He thought of Anna, who had social studies first period (he'd figured out her schedule), and wondered what would happen to her. Would she be scared? He hoped he and Claudia could keep their faces straight, act confused, and play along with everyone else.

But they never got the chance.

About ten minutes into the lesson, as Reynolds was

building to a point about the poem they were discussing, they heard sirens.

At first Jeremy thought the sirens were going past the school. Maybe there was a fire somewhere. But they grew louder and louder. One of the girls by the window gasped and pointed, and Reynolds left the board to look. Everyone stood up, craning their necks to see, and Jeremy was drawn out of his seat to look himself.

Fire trucks and an ambulance were parked at crazy angles all over the front lawn of the school.

Jeremy and Claudia looked at each other. And all Jeremy could think was, *Oh no.*

# TWENTY

**HALF THE CLASS WAS GAWKING OUT THE WINDOW**
and whispering when Reynolds, after a moment of shock, snapped back into action. "Class!" he said sharply. "Back to your seats!"

The girls—and Jeremy—reluctantly returned to their places as Reynolds dialed the classroom phone.

As Jeremy sank into his chair, panic swelled inside his chest. What was going on? Was it a fire? The doors were locked. If the school was actually on fire, everyone would be trapped. Because of him. He tried to take a breath but couldn't get any air.

Reynolds waited a minute at the phone, silent, then hung up. He addressed the class again. "I need to go to the office and find out what's going on. I want you all to stay in your seats unless another adult tells you to leave the classroom. Do you understand?"

The girls nodded, but Jeremy could barely hear what the teacher was saying.

Reynolds strode to the door. The world seemed to

change into slow motion. The teacher reached out a hand, put it on the door handle, and tried to turn the knob.

But nothing happened. He paused, shook his head, then strode quickly to the rear of the room and tried the little-used back door, but that one was locked as well.

"What the . . ." He trailed off.

The full story didn't come out until much later, after the firefighters had gone through the building to release the frantic students and sent everyone home for the day.

The moments Jeremy sat waiting for those firefighters were the longest of his life. His mind veered wildly from one potential disaster to another. Class wasn't over yet, so why all the panic? And why was there an actual ambulance outside? It was only a few doorknobs! Just a harmless prank . . .

More than any other time, even when Rachel got suspended, Jeremy wished he could reverse the clock. Right back to the day Andrew Marks left and he first got himself into this mess.

At dinner Jeremy's mother let loose with an infuriated tirade. She had been stuck at school late, as had all the teachers and staff, in a long and angry meeting.

"This is all Powell's fault," she said. "She kept encouraging this garbage, kept letting it go with a wink and a nod, and now you see what happens. Somebody actually got hurt. The board should have her head for this."

As it turned out, the gaggle of girls who normally held court in the downstairs bathroom every morning were all on the volleyball team, something Jeremy hadn't remembered until it was too late. They were in Vermont that day, at the tournament. Only one girl had entered the bathroom before first period: Bethany Howland, or, as Claudia called her, Weezer.

"That's not really fair," Tabitha had said the first time the nickname came up. "I have asthma too, and it's nothing to make fun of."

"It's not because she has asthma," Claudia had insisted. "It's because of the band! She reminds me of the lead singer."

"Yeah, right. I'm not an idiot," Tabitha said. But Claudia stuck to her story.

Bethany had gone to the first floor girl's bathroom to use the toilet. Afterward, she checked her hair in the mirror and then tried to get out of the bathroom to head to her first class. But the door had locked itself. She tried calling for help, but no one heard her in the hustle and bustle of the hallway outside.

Being locked in the bathroom alone made her feel claustrophobic (as she reported to the paramedics). Feeling claustrophobic made her panic. And being panicky triggered an asthma attack, a major one.

But she had left her inhaler in her locker.

Freaking out, she tried to call her friends on the cell phone she carried for emergencies. Of course they were all in classes, cell phones off, as per school rules. So she called her mother at work, but only got voice mail.

Finally, in desperation, she called 911.

"What else could the poor girl do?" Jeremy's mother asked. "Who knew how long she would be in there. And it was good that she did, too, because you were all locked in. Even if she had been able to get someone on the phone, they wouldn't have been able to help her. What a disaster. We're lucky someone wasn't seriously hurt. What if there had been a fire?"

Jeremy tried to arrange his face into an appropriately horrified expression. And the truth was, he *was* horrified. Just not for the same reasons as his mother.

"What happened next?" Jane asked. She'd been on a class field trip and missed the whole thing.

"It was mayhem, absolute insanity," their mother said. "Once the fire trucks and ambulances came, all the teachers tried to get out of their classrooms to see what was going on, and of course they couldn't. And because the fire trucks came everyone thought there was an actual fire! They were banging on the doors, calling to the firefighters. It took ages before everyone figured out what had happened and how to fix it, and by then the firefighters had broken half the locks. It's going to cost I don't know how much to replace everything. What a waste."

"So do they know who did it?" Jane asked. "They know it couldn't be Rachel and the team, right?"

Jeremy's mother shook her head. "Of course. Even Powell admitted that. So hopefully she'll get that suspension off her record, even if they did miss participating in the tournament. If anything good could come of this, that would be it."

"What happened to the girl?" Jane asked.

"She went to the hospital for observation," their mother said. "She'll be fine, thankfully. And I guess they're getting someone in tonight to change all the doorknobs so nothing like this can ever happen again."

"So, all's well that ends well?" Jeremy knew it was the wrong thing to say even before the words left his mouth.

His mother stared at him. "I don't know what's wrong with you, Jeremy. A girl could have died today, all because of a stupid prank. Died! Alone! Locked in a bathroom."

Looking at her angry face, Jeremy felt small and young. He hadn't thought something serious would happen, that someone like Bethany could really get hurt. Not hurting anyone was one of the rules. And it was all because of Whitey's prank. And Jeremy's, a little voice in his head reminded him. He was the one who did the bathroom, everyone else just did classrooms. Nobody was alone in a classroom.

# TWENTY-ONE

**THE NEXT MORNING AT ASSEMBLY DIRECTOR** Powell was as grave as Jeremy had ever seen her. There was no more reference to a band of merry pranksters at St. Edith's, no more winks and nods. Instead she soberly discussed the incident and its ramifications as the students sat in grim silence.

"It's gone too far," Powell said. "I don't know who is responsible for these pranks, but this behavior has got to stop. And we are going to find the perpetrators, I promise you."

That afternoon Jeremy and Claudia went to Mickey's to meet up with Whitey, who seemed excited to see them until he saw the glum expressions on their faces. "That bad, huh?"

Jeremy had felt subdued all day at school, like he was walking under water. He didn't know what he was supposed to feel; all he knew was that he felt worse than he ever had before. And he barely listened when Claudia told Whitey the whole story.

"We're just lucky it wasn't worse," she finished up. "There were ambulances and everything!"

"But who changed the lock on the bathroom?" Whitey wanted to know. "I thought we were only doing classrooms."

"I did," Jeremy said grimly. "I thought it would be funny."

"Well, it's not like you could have known," Claudia said. "Of all the people to go in there by herself and get locked in!"

Jeremy shook his head. He'd never thought he would say this, but for once he agreed with Director Powell. They'd gone too far.

But Claudia seemed undeterred, bemused even, by the turn of events. "We could keep doing pranks, you know," she said. "Not to get kicked out—but maybe as a film project? Something just for the two of us? I actually have another great idea, but we're going to need some fireworks. Don't worry—we just have to go to New Hampshire."

"New Hampshire?"

"It's okay; don't freak out. Ian will drive us. I'll promise to write him another paper. We'll tell your mother we're going to the mall or something."

"Claudia . . ."

She laughed. "Don't be a wimp. It'll be great. And we won't get caught."

"But what about the rules? Things got broken! Someone was hurt!" He couldn't stop thinking about it. He'd done exactly what he'd said he didn't want to do—broken all of his own rules. And now Claudia wanted to do something with fireworks? That was much more dangerous than an asthma attack.

"Not really hurt. She had an asthma attack. She has them like nine times a day in gym class," she said. "But anyway, nobody is going to get hurt this time. We were a little sloppy before, so we just have to be more careful."

"And the lobby? It's basically destroyed. And the computer lab . . ."

"Oh, you know how they do things around here," Claudia said with a wave of her hand. "Somebody will make a big donation. We don't even have to get in trouble."

"You think money solves everything!"

"Well, sorry, but sometimes it does."

He looked away from her. Part of him knew she was right, and he hated her for it. She didn't have to go to St. Edith's because her parents couldn't afford to send her anywhere else. She didn't have to be Rachel, stressed out and perfect, hoping for a scholarship. She'd be able to go to any school in the state; her dad just had to write a check. Meanwhile Jeremy was lucky if his dad sent enough child support to cover his books and uniforms.

This whole process was leaving a terrible taste in his mouth. He felt like a really bad person, someone who didn't care what happened to other people. He hated that his mother was so horrified by the pranks, and it made him shudder to think what would happen once she found out it had been him all along.

Even going to St. Edith's for the rest of his life would be better than the disappointment and anger from everyone who cared about him. He didn't want to be the only boy at school, but he still wanted to be himself, to be Jeremy. And these pranks, people getting hurt . . . they just weren't him.

"I just can't, Claudia," he said finally. "It's over."

She shook her head. "You have to realize that even if you never do another prank again, they're going to find out," she said ominously. "We've left enough tracks behind: your mittens, the fact that your mom has keys to the school. If they really want to know, they will."

"I'm sorry," he said. "But I can't do this anymore."

"Well, then," she said, getting up. "I guess I've been doing all of this for nothing, huh? Great. I could have been editing my movie or even doing homework, but no, I've been helping you! And this is what I get as payback."

"Oh, poor you," Jeremy said with sudden anger. "I forgot—it's all about you. Come on, Claudia, do you really always have to be the center of everything?"

"I DO NOT ALWAYS HAVE TO BE THE CENTER OF EVERYTHING."

Even Quasimodo looked up at that.

"Guys, come on," Whitey said. "Don't take it out on each other."

Jeremy ignored him. "Oh right. So you're just yelling in the middle of a public place . . . I dunno, LIKE SOMEONE WHO HAS TO BE THE CENTER OF EVERYTHING." And now he was yelling, and people were looking at him, but it didn't feel weird or embarrassing, it felt liberating. Like the feeling he got after a successful prank. In fact, he felt like yelling some more. "WHY DON'T YOU BUTT OUT OF MY LIFE? And by the way, don't worry about my problems affecting your stupid movie. Because I QUIT."

Claudia opened her mouth like she was going to say something, then stopped, then started again. But when she finally spoke, she wasn't yelling anymore. "Fine," she said, pulling on her coat and grabbing her bag off the table. "Whatever." She stalked to the front of the restaurant and opened the door, then turned back. Her voice sounded hurt and heavy, and very un-Claudia. All she said was, "Sometimes you really stink."

Then she walked out.

Jeremy crumpled up the potato chip packet in front of him as noisily as possible, but it wasn't remotely satisfying. He wanted to punch something. He stood up and kicked the recycling bin, but it only made a very unsatisfying thump.

"Wow, that was harsh," Whitey said from the table. "But she'll get over it, I'm sure."

Jeremy knew he was trying to be comforting but Whitey really had no idea. *Clueless fool,* Jeremy thought, *with his stupid ideas for pranks.*

"Why are you always hanging around us?" Jeremy asked savagely.

Whitey looked insulted. "Well, sorry," he said. "Sorry for thinking I was helping, or something."

"You didn't help! You ruined everything!" Jeremy said. "We're going to get in huge trouble now."

"I thought that was what you wanted," Whitey shot back. "Besides, I never told you to switch the doorknob on a bathroom. Just classrooms."

He was right. It had been Jeremy's idea to fix the bathroom, because of the smug and mysterious girls who disappeared through that door. He took a deep breath. He wasn't angry at Whitey. He wasn't even really angry at Claudia. Mainly he was angry with himself.

"I know," he said, changing his tone. "It's not your fault. It's not even your school. It's mine. I started all of this and dragged Claudia into it."

"Why did you even want to get kicked out of St. Edith's?" Whitey asked. "It's a good school, and it seems like you've got a solid deal, going for free and everything. You'll probably get to go to one of the private high schools, too. Why try and ruin it?"

"I'm sick of being surrounded by all girls," Jeremy said. "And don't say it. I know what you're thinking; it's what everybody says. But trust me, it's nothing like people expect. It's not the same. I just want to have some guy friends, that's all."

Whitey gave him a funny look. "Aren't we friends?"

"Yeah," Jeremy said after a brief pause. "Of course." He felt like an idiot. Like more than an idiot. He'd been hanging out with this guy more than he'd ever hung out with Andrew Marks or any of the other boys who used to go to St. Edith's.

Jeremy looked at Whitey almost like he had never really seen him before. It seemed like Whitey—Dylan—was turning into a friend, instead of a random kid who hung around Mickey's. A guy friend. He wondered how he'd missed that.

"Besides, Harding kind of stinks," Whitey continued. "I don't know why you'd want to go there. You're a nice guy, but you'd probably get beaten up, like, every day the first couple of weeks."

"Really?" Jeremy asked. "I mean, for real?" He'd had his reservations about going to Harding, and his mom had talked enough about how bad it was academically, but he hadn't thought about it actually being worse, really worse, for him than being the only boy at St. Edith's. What if he didn't make any friends, at all, ever? What if he did get beaten up by the other boys, like Whitey said?

"Well, at least if you do get kicked out and sent to Harding, you'll know somebody," Whitey offered. But Jeremy barely heard.

# TWENTY-TWO

**THE NEXT DAY CLAUDIA WOULDN'T SPEAK TO** him. It wasn't the first time she'd given him the silent treatment, but this time she wasn't being dramatic about it, just quiet and a little bit sad. He wondered what she was most upset about, him quitting the movie or what he'd said about her and the pranks. And since he'd quit the movie, he didn't get to see Anna all day, but somehow that didn't seem to matter that much. He felt numb.

After dinner he wandered over to Emily's—though she hadn't been all that happy with him either lately. He wondered if he could be happy with his life—and with St. Edith's—if things with his two best friends just went back to normal.

Emily was in her room doing homework. He wanted to talk to her, to tell her everything that was going on, but it seemed too complicated. So all he said was, "Claudia and I had a fight."

"What else is new?" she replied placidly.

"We don't fight that much!"

"Yes, you do," she said. "It's one of the reasons why I don't think you guys are good as friends."

Oh great, now Emily was going to start in on Claudia. But she paused, and then added, "What was the fight about this time?"

"It's hard to explain," he said. "It was nothing, really, just a fight."

"Was it about the prank?"

He stared at her. "What do you mean?"

"Well, Bethany had to go to the hospital; that's kind of a big deal," Emily said.

"And . . ."

"Come on, Jeremy." She rolled her eyes. "You keep denying it, but I know it was you. You and Claudia and Anna and Tabitha and Delaney, your whole little band of Merry Pranksters, right? And now it all blew up in your faces, and Claudia's mad at you even though it was all probably her idea in the first place. Am I right?"

Jeremy felt oddly panicked. He hadn't really thought about what would happen if Emily figured out who was behind the pranks. Would she turn him in? A few weeks ago he might have been glad that Emily had figured it out.

It would have been easy for her to go to Powell and tell. But now he just wanted to convince her to keep his secret.

"Let me guess," Emily said, making a face at him. "You're sitting there thinking, 'Woe is me. I wish I had guy friends I could really talk to about this,' aren't you?"

"No," he said. "Well, maybe."

"You do realize that you're sitting here talking to me about all these things, and I am technically a girl the last time I checked?"

"I know," he said.

"So what is it that you're looking for, Jeremy? I think you've built up this idea of guy friends to the point where you don't have a grip on reality. I know, I know. You have no frame of reference—poor little Jeremy stuck in the land of the Amazons. But, really, have you met any guys recently? What do you think you'd talk about with them? Your truest innermost self? Did you talk about stuff like that with Andrew Marks?"

"No, but Andrew Marks is an idiot," he said reflexively. But he thought about Whitey and it occurred to him that the fact that he didn't get along with other guys was maybe more *his* problem.

"All boys are idiots, Jeremy," Emily said.

"I'm not."

"Maybe that has more to do with you always hanging out with girls. Have you ever thought about that?"

"Okay, Emily one, Jeremy zero. But I'm sorry. I still want to be a normal kid, not some kind of freak. I just want to fit in. Is that a weird thing to want? Doesn't everybody want that?"

"Fine, then, get yourself kicked out of school. Forget about all your friends. Go to Harding and be happy. See if we care." She sighed.

"It's not like that!"

"It is, though, isn't it?" she said. "If what you want is something more, that means what you have is not enough, and that's never nice to hear."

"It's not personal," he said. "Besides, I don't want to go to Harding anymore. I just want everything to go back to normal."

"Well, good, because I hate to see you keep acting like an idiot," she said. "Besides, who knows? Maybe you've been wrong all along. Maybe St. Edith's is where you really belong."

⇨

For the next couple of days Claudia still didn't speak to him—a record, since usually her best efforts rarely lasted longer than a day. And while Tabitha and Delaney were pleasant enough, it was awkward to sit with them at lunch when Claudia so pointedly didn't include him in the conversation. Being ignored by Claudia was more troubling than he had expected. It made him feel off-kilter, like the world had shifted and he was the only one standing in the same place.

By Friday morning he was antsy and anxious. He felt like something bad was going to happen and he was powerless to stop it. Bad karma, his mother called it.

He had tried to get kicked out of school, and people got hurt, including his own sister, though the last prank had made them reconsider her role in everything. But now one of his best friends was mad at him, and he might actually get in major trouble. His mother said they were "investigating" the doorknob prank. He had no idea what that meant—fingerprints? Lie detector tests?—but he knew it wasn't going to end well.

Even when he passed Anna in the hall and she gave

him a little wave, his mood didn't improve. All he could think was what she, and everyone else, would do when they realized all of this was his fault. The heady thrill of getting away with something had been replaced by a ball of dread, deep in the bottom of his stomach.

Friday, instead of going down to the awkward cafeteria, he took his sandwich and drink to the band room, where he knew he could find an empty corner to eat in.

But it wasn't empty; Mr. Reynolds was sitting at a computer near the back. They had moved a few of the surviving machines from the basement to different classrooms while waiting for the computer lab to be repaired, and one had ended up in the band room.

"Oh, hi," he said when he spotted Jeremy. "What are you up to?"

"Just wanted to find a quiet place to eat my lunch and study for a test," he said, half-truthfully.

"Oh, well, I won't be long in here," Reynolds said. "I was burning some copies of the *Mission to Mercury* movie so Ms. Powell and a few of the board members could watch it at home. We can't screen it for the school without their approval."

"Cool," Jeremy said. He guessed Claudia had finally finished the movie without him. Maybe she'd used some of the outtakes with him in them, or maybe she'd cut him out completely. He told himself he didn't really care, dropped into a chair as far from the teacher as possible, and started poking around in his lunch bag.

But then Reynolds stood up and said, "Wait, Jeremy." For a horrifying moment Jeremy thought he was going to talk about his mother.

But instead Reynolds walked around the table and stood a few chairs down from where Jeremy sat, his unwrapped sandwich in his lap. "I hope I'm not overstepping my bounds, but I wanted to see how you were holding up. I know it has to be hard, being the only boy in school."

Jeremy gave a forced laugh. "Nobody else seems to think so."

"Well, that's because they're all girls," Reynolds said, and then Jeremy really laughed.

"The thing is, your mom talked to me a little bit about you wanting to go to another school. And as much as I'd hate to see such a good student leave, I'm not entirely convinced that's a bad idea."

"Really?" This was unexpected.

"It can't be good for your mental health, standing out so much," Reynolds said. "I know I would have been completely unequipped to handle it at your age. Though I have to admit, overall I've been impressed. A lot of boys wouldn't have been able to make friends at all."

"Thanks," Jeremy said. He was surprised. He never thought of himself as handling anything well, least of all day-to-day life at St. Edith's. For a brief moment he wondered what his father would say. Did he think Jeremy handled things well? Or did he even know Jeremy well enough to judge?

"Some of the other boys here were completely miserable," Reynolds said. "Andrew Marks was in really bad shape by the time he transferred. He seemed to think all the girls hated him and were always gossiping behind his back."

Well, that was technically true. Though hearing it put that way made Jeremy feel a little bit sorry for Andrew, a novel sensation.

"So, I suppose what I'm asking is, are you okay?" Reynolds continued. He looked at Jeremy closely. "Because you seem fine, but appearances can be deceiving."

Jeremy considered this question for a minute. Part of him knew if he told Reynolds he was unhappy, the teacher would report back to Jeremy's mother and maybe, just maybe, sway her into letting him transfer somewhere else.

But in his heart he knew even if he could switch to someplace like MacArthur Prep, there wasn't any guarantee it would be better than St. Edith's. There would still be good things and bad things, fun days and not-so-fun days. The more he thought about it, the more he wondered if what he wanted from another school even really existed.

Maybe his problem was more him than anything else.

"I don't know," he said finally. "Sometimes I am; sometimes I'm not. But I'd probably be like that anywhere."

"That's a wise observation," Reynolds said. "But I wouldn't expect any less from you. Anyway, I'll leave you to your lunch."

"Thanks," Jeremy said. He remembered Emily saying Reynolds was really good to talk to, and now he felt like he understood why. "I mean it."

# TWENTY-THREE

**SUNDAY NIGHT THE DOORBELL RANG WHILE** Jeremy was unloading the dishwasher after dinner. His mom was sitting at the kitchen table going over some bills. All weekend he'd been waiting for something horrible to happen—a phone call from Powell? Police at the door?— so his stomach lurched.

A moment later Jeremy's sister ushered Claudia into the kitchen.

She looked like she hadn't slept in days, and she wasn't wearing a coat, only a long, shapeless cardigan. She must have been freezing, walking all the way from Red Mill.

"Sorry, I know it's late," she said to Jeremy's mother. "But can I talk to Jeremy?"

"Sure, sweetheart," his mother said, and gave Jeremy a pointed look, like he'd done something wrong.

"Let's go out back," Jeremy said. He grabbed some coats from the closet, one for him and one for Claudia, and led her out into the yard. It was cold, but at least there was privacy.

When they were settled on the Adirondack chairs, Jeremy asked, "So what's up?"

"Ian gave me a ride," she said, as though that explained everything.

He nodded.

"I'm sorry I yelled at you," she said, looking out at the trees. "It's just . . . I thought you were my friend."

"Well, I am," he said. "But that doesn't mean I run around doing everything you say."

"Doesn't it?" she said with a wicked smile. She sounded like herself, and in a rush he realized, annoying as she was sometimes, he really did miss her when she wasn't around.

"I'm sorry I quit the movie," he said.

"That's okay. We had enough footage, with the special effects. It turned out . . . fine, I guess. We'll see at the screening. Powell signed off, so there's going to be a special assembly tomorrow for the whole school. I just wish . . ." Here she trailed off.

"Wish what?"

She made a grumbly little noise, half like a sigh. "I wish we could have done it together, is all. I keep thinking that if you get caught and leave St. Edith's soon, we won't have Film Club, or any of it."

Jeremy started to speak, but she held up her hand. "And I'm fine with that, okay? I get it. I understand you want to be normal, and who am I to judge? I've never been the only girl at school. I have no clue what you're going through. I pretend I do, but I don't, really."

He allowed himself a small smile at that, but it was clear she wasn't finished.

"Only, lately I feel like everything's changing. And I hate that." She looked off again. "You'll be at the public school, hanging out with kids I don't even know—boys— and then you'll feel weird being best friends with a girl. And then we'll all go off to high school, probably different ones. It's never going to be the same again, is it? It'll be like I don't even know you anymore."

Jeremy took a deep breath. "The thing is, *I* don't even know me anymore," he said. "If I'm not the kid in the movies and I'm not the kid who does pranks and I'm not the kid who plays sports or is in a cool band, either, then . . ."

"Then what? Then you're just you, which is better

than all of that. Well, except being the guy in my movies, that's the best thing," she said, but he could tell she was joking. Sort of.

"What if they find out about the pranks and I get kicked out and I'm still not happy? What happens if I'm not happy anywhere?" It was the big question, one he hadn't wanted to even ask himself. But he was slowly beginning to realize that he was the only one who could answer that—not boys his own age, or his missing dad, or even a girl like Anna. It was up to him.

The crazy thing—the thing he couldn't tell Claudia because she'd probably laugh—was that sitting in his yard, the tip of his nose practically frozen and his ungloved hands in his pockets, he was actually happy. Happy to be sitting with his best friend, with his family safe inside, and having things feel like they were getting back to normal. He hated fighting with Claudia, and honestly, as much fun as he'd had doing the pranks, it had really been more about hanging out with his best friend. He'd always wanted things to be normal, but maybe this was what normal was.

"Wanna watch a movie, or something?" he asked her.

LEE GJERTSEN MALONE

She was shivering; they would need to go inside any minute.

"Sure," she said. "But I get to pick."

"You always get to pick," he protested.

"And this is a surprise because . . . ?" she asked. They both laughed.

# TWENTY-FOUR

**ON MONDAY, JEREMY FELT BETTER THAN HE HAD** in a while. He and Claudia had patched things up, and it seemed as if he could put the pranks behind him and just get on with life. Seventh grade was almost half over. Eighth grade couldn't possibly be worse, right? Maybe someday he'd be able to look back and laugh at his time at a not-quite-all-girls school. Heck, by high school he might even be able to spin it so the other guys were jealous.

That morning he went straight to his locker, lost in his thoughts. So if the girls he passed stared or giggled more than usual, he didn't notice.

He took extra time getting his books, figuring he'd get to morning assembly as late as possible and sit at the back. Not attracting any attention seemed like the best way to separate himself from all the excitement and questions surrounding the pranks. He wondered where Claudia was. Probably off preparing for the *Mission to Mercury* screening, which was supposed to happen that afternoon at a special assembly.

That's when he noticed the poster taped to the wall next to his locker.

At first he thought it had something to do with the movie. But it didn't look like a movie poster at all. It looked like a poster for a rock band. By why would a band poster be taped on a wall in the middle of a hallway at St. Edith's Academy?

He peered more closely at the poster and was shocked to see his own face looking back.

His own face, but not on his own body. Instead it had been pasted or photoshopped onto a picture of some crazy seventies-style rock star, with skintight satin pants and a shirt half open, chest hair pouring out, playing a guitar, and surrounded by girls. What the heck?

He ripped it down. Above the picture were bubbly letters saying *The Merry Pranksters!* with lots of exclamation points. The Merry Pranksters. That's what Powell had called the kids doing the pranks. And below that it said "St. Edith's Best (and Only) Rock Band."

A rock band? He looked at the girls in the picture and gulped. Next to the picture of him was a girl, a woman really, in a bikini.

But her face. Her face was unmistakably Anna's.

Oh no. He scanned the rest of the poster, his heart beating faster and faster. Behind him were three other girls dressed as rock stars—Delaney, Tabitha, and Claudia.

*Claudia.*

He tore off down the hall, hoping and wishing it was the only poster, a little joke on him, but of course it wasn't. He saw dozens of them—pinned on bulletin boards, taped to lockers, and even stuck on the glass door to the stairwell. He ripped down one after another, stalking faster and faster down the hall, pulling them down, crumpling them in his fists.

Only one person in the whole world could possibly, would even *dare*, pull off a prank like this.

*Claudia.*

As he ran, he thought of Anna and what she would think when she saw the posters. His anger burned as his thoughts turned to Claudia. She had seemed so understanding last night, so sincere. But it had all been a lie. And for what? To have their old friendship back the way it was, with him as her little sidekick, doing her bidding and keeping his mouth shut? Did she really think he would put up with this because she had said she missed him?

As he grabbed poster after poster, he saw passing girls staring at him, laughing at him, but he didn't care. Maybe he could get all the posters down before everyone saw them. Before Anna saw them.

He ran down the stairs, ripping down posters as he went. Claudia must have made dozens, even hundreds. They were everywhere.

Then he skidded around a corner and stopped short, because Anna was standing by herself at a locker, looking at something.

She glanced up at the squeal of his rubber heels skidding to a halt on the smooth hall floor. She seemed shocked at first, then composed herself.

"What is this?" she demanded, waving one of the posters at him. "Is this supposed to be funny?"

"No." He could barely get the words out through the lump in his throat. "Or yes. I don't know."

"Why would you do something like this?" She seemed genuinely confused and hurt. "I've never done anything to you. I'm new here, and I joined Film Club to make friends, and now you go and make something like this?"

She stared at him, her face crumpled in anger. "I

thought you guys liked me, and now I find out you've all been laughing at me behind my back."

"I wouldn't—I didn't—"

"What is everybody going to think when they see this, that I'm some kind of . . . I don't even know. And my mom is coming to see the movie today. She's going to freak." She was shaking her head, not even looking at him. "I've never done anything to you."

"I know . . . I . . . didn't . . ." But he couldn't get the words out.

She ripped the poster into a dozen tiny pieces, threw them at his feet, and walked away.

# TWENTY-FIVE

**JEREMY CUT MORNING ASSEMBLY AND HID IN THE** band room, after he'd torn down all the posters he could find and stuffed their remains in the Dumpster behind the school. He wanted to cut language arts, too, but he knew Reynolds would definitely tell his mom.

His mom. He'd been so worried about Anna seeing the posters he hadn't thought about what would happen when his mom did. Would she figure it out? Would she guess it was him behind all those pranks? Would she think he made a habit of putting the faces of girls from school on bikini pictures on his computer? She was going to really kill him this time, tear him up like one of the posters he'd destroyed and leave him for dead. He was sure of it.

In Reynolds's class he settled into his seat and closed his eyes, trying to ignore the whispers around him. He didn't need to listen hard to figure out what they were talking about.

Right before the bell, Claudia slid into her seat next

to him and whispered, in a faux comforting tone, "Tough morning, huh, tiger?"

Jeremy opened his eyes but didn't look at her. Instead he stared straight ahead. Claudia thought she could get away with anything when it came to him, but not this time. Maybe he wasn't cut out for a life of crime, but he wasn't a doormat, either. "I guess you think you're hilarious."

"Sorry, just trying to lighten the mood."

He shook his head. "Yeah, well, thanks a lot," he said in a sarcastic hiss.

"Hey!" she said. "Don't get all mad at me. I didn't do anything."

That was beyond the pale, even for her. "Oh, come off it, Claudia. I know you made those posters. Who else would pull a prank like that?"

She stared at him. Reynolds had come in and was taking papers out of his briefcase. "Do you really think I would do something like that?" she asked slowly. "Really?"

"Anna hates me now, thanks to you. And I'm going to get in serious trouble."

"You're certifiable. I would never do that. Your mom

works at the school! When she finds out, she'll kill you. And the rules of the pranks—nobody is supposed to get hurt."

"Like you ever cared about that before."

He opened a notebook and turned his shoulder so he couldn't see her. She made a noise like she was going to speak again, but a look from Reynolds made her think better of it.

Reynolds moved in front of the board. "Okay, class, settle down."

When class was over, Claudia spoke to Jeremy once more. "Fine, if that's how it's going to be, what do I care?"

He let out a mean laugh. "Yeah, what do you care about me?"

And left.

Jeremy traveled through his morning classes in a daze, not even thinking about the school assembly that afternoon for the *Mission to Mercury* screening. He'd been waiting all day for the loudspeaker to come to life, telling him to report to the director's office, but it never did. Maybe, he thought wildly, Powell would see this as another prank helping the school's reputation. But somehow he doubted it.

He managed to keep his head down and avoid everyone until the screening, which he hoped to miss completely by hiding in the band room again. But as he walked quickly past the auditorium he heard a sharp voice call his name.

His mother.

"Where do you think you're going?" she asked, grabbing his arm.

"I, uh." He had nothing.

"You're sitting with me," she said, steering him through the door into the auditorium. From the clawlike grip of her hand, it was clear that she had seen the poster.

A sixth grader handed them programs, the ones Emily had taken pictures for that day he tried to talk to Anna and ended up telling her all those stupid lies. It seemed ages ago. He was pretty sure she wouldn't care whether or not he was in a band now.

They walked down the aisle toward the front of the auditorium, which slowly filled with students. His mother smiled when they spotted Reynolds sitting in the front row, and to Jeremy's horror he waved them over.

When they sat down, Jeremy waited, almost holding his breath, for his mother to say something, but she immediately turned and started chatting with Reynolds in an infuriatingly animated way. So he flipped through the program, gazing at all the faces—his own, Anna's, and the people he had believed were his friends—but he found it hard to focus.

"Mom," he finally said, touching her arm. "Come on. Won't you at least talk to me?"

She turned and looked at him. "Fine. Talk."

"Not like that," he pleaded.

"Like what? What do you want me to say? I'm proud of you? Because trust me, I'm not. If this is true, if you actually did all those pranks—well, then I'm really disappointed in you, Jeremy."

"I know," he said, miserable.

"After this . . . screening or whatever it is, you and I have to go down to Ms. Powell's office for a little chat with her," she said. "I suppose you know what that probably means?"

He nodded dumbly. Of course his mother would be there if he was getting expelled. Parents always got called in when their kids were in major trouble, not that people often got into major trouble at St. Edith's. And his mother didn't even have to leave work.

She was still talking, but there was a catch in her throat. "Look, I'm doing the best I can, okay? It's not easy being a single mother. You guys don't give me enough credit for trying, like everything I do is the worst thing in the world. And now you hang posters of yourself acting crazy all over the school?"

"Stop it," he said. "Stop . . . blaming yourself." He hated when she did this—took the burden of everything on her own shoulders—but it struck him it was also a way of making all his problems about her. He'd never thought of that before.

"I just wish I understood why, Jeremy," his mother said. "Why get in trouble now? When you've only got a year and a half left until you get a scholarship to any high school you want?"

He took a deep breath. "I never wanted to be the last boy."

"Is it really that terrible? That you'd try to get yourself into trouble?"

"You wouldn't let me transfer," he said petulantly.

She closed her eyes. "I'm sorry, but you have to understand. I can't let you change schools. You know this."

For a minute he thought she might cry, but all she said was, "I'm sorry you're so unhappy."

"I'm not," he said. "I'm really not."

"Then what the heck were you thinking?"

He let the question hang there, as the lights began to dim and the audience began shushing itself. He didn't know what he'd been thinking. All he knew was that now he was unhappier than he'd ever been, and none of it had to do with being the last boy.

He didn't want to think about what was going to happen in Powell's office that afternoon, so he forced his attention to the screen. He had to admit, even with everything that had happened, he was a teeny bit curious about the film itself. He'd only seen a few snippets on Claudia's computer. He had no idea what the final product would be like.

White words scrolled against an inky sky, like in *Star Wars*. Jeremy smiled to himself, knowing Claudia had probably added the reference just for him. Then he shook his head. He had to remember he was furious with her.

As it turned out, the movie itself was pretty terrible. The plot was garbled, the special effects campy. But somehow, against all odds, Claudia had managed to capture something of the energy of the performers, something that made the audience connect. They laughed at all the right places and in only a few wrong ones. They gasped at the fight scene with the neutron swords and clapped when the villains were vanquished and said "ahhh" when Captain Flynn and Dr. Zizmor finally admitted their love.

And it wasn't as hard as he thought, watching himself on the screen with Anna, even though he was sure she hated him now. They were so clearly characters in a movie it was like it wasn't even them at all.

"That was pretty good," his mother said when it was finished.

"You sound surprised," Jeremy said.

"I'm not, actually. You and Claudia work well together."

"Yeah."

He didn't want to get up, didn't want to walk down the hall to Powell's office. But his mother picked up her purse. "I have to check my messages. I'll see you in Powell's office in fifteen minutes. Don't be late."

# TWENTY-SIX

**HE WAITED UNTIL MOST STUDENTS HAD LEFT THE** theater. He wanted to avoid Claudia, who was probably standing right outside the doors being congratulated by everyone. He couldn't stomach that right now.

When he finally headed out, Emily was lurking in the shadows in the back of the theater. He stopped and gave her a small smile.

"You look terrible," she said.

"Do I? Maybe because I'm about to get kicked out of school."

She gave him a weird look. "I thought that's what you wanted," she said. "Besides, aren't you supposed to be standing out front with Claudia having people tell you how wonderful you are?"

"Claudia," he said with as much venom as he could muster. "Why would I want to go stand with her? I thought she was my best friend, but she's trying to ruin my life."

"How did Claudia try to ruin your life?" Emily asked.

"Come on, Emily, didn't you see those posters? They were all over school."

"You don't think *she* made them, do you?" Emily said slowly.

"Who else could it be?"

"I don't know. Claudia Hoffmann can't be the only person at St. Edith's who can come up with a prank." Her voice had taken on a weird tone.

"What are you trying to say?"

Emily laughed, short and hard. "I don't get you, Jeremy. One minute you and your friends are excited about pulling all sorts of crazy pranks on the school, but the minute somebody plays one on you, it's the worst thing in the world. I guess this prank wasn't cool enough or something?"

"The rules were that nobody was supposed to get hurt. Or humiliated. But people did get hurt. Anna's mad and hates me."

"Well, maybe precious Anna should have realized what you were like before she started hanging out with you."

Jeremy laughed in spite of himself. "You think I've been hanging out with Anna? Hilarious."

"Playing pranks," Emily said, rolling her eyes at him. "It's obvious you like her, so of course you'd invite her along. She's new and exciting and cool, not like lame old me."

"I don't think you're lame," he said, but even as the words were coming out he was painfully aware of how many times he'd thought exactly that.

"Of course you do," she said. "Boring old Emily, good for doing homework with, but never anything wild or fun."

He stared at her in amazement. Was she saying she wanted to play pranks?

"You just don't get it," she said, turning like she was going to leave. "Well, I'm sorry if you get kicked out of school . . . if that's not what you want."

She left, and he looked down again at the program in his hand, the one Emily had designed. He stared at the headshots of faces, and they all looked achingly familiar, like he'd seen them before. Dozens of times, in fact.

"Emily!" he shouted, and ran after her. "Emily!"

"What?" she said, barely stopping.

"Did you . . . You did . . ." He was a little out of breath, from nerves and from the sudden burst of running. "But I would never think . . ."

Emily didn't look at him. "Of course you wouldn't. It's never me, is it?"

"But . . . but how could you?"

She shook her head. "I thought it was funny. Aren't pranks supposed to be funny?"

He stared at her. It hadn't been Claudia. Claudia would never do something like this. She knew the rules. And as mad as she was about him bailing on the pranks and quitting the movie, she was his friend. She'd come over only the day before to talk things out. How could he have blamed Claudia for this? How could he not have known?

He shook his head. "I thought we were friends, Emily. I thought you cared about me."

"I do care about you," she said. Her voice caught, and he was suddenly terrified she might start crying. "Can't you see? We used to do everything together! We have so much in common. Don't you know? Or are you that stupid?"

He didn't know, and now he didn't know what to say.

"It's in every movie. The guy who has known the girl his entire life, and one day he looks at her and he sees someone completely different. Isn't that how life is supposed to work?" She laughed, but it wasn't a happy sound.

"I see how you look at that girl. I know what you're thinking. But what I don't understand is why?" She stared at him like she was trying to read words written on the inside of his skull. "Why her?"

She didn't say it, but he could see the rest in her eyes, the part that said, *And not me.*

"I don't know," he answered honestly.

He remembered her talking about the uncanny valley, that point where an animated character looked too much like a person, and he thought maybe his relationship with Emily had an uncanny valley too. A point where things got too weird. Maybe people were right. Maybe he had been using her.

He didn't know if he was mad or sorry. Or both.

And then the loudspeaker started up, so loud his whole body jerked. "Jeremy Miner, please report to the director's office immediately. Jeremy Miner."

# TWENTY-SEVEN

**JEREMY WALKED TO THE OFFICE SLOWLY, DREAD-**ing every step. He hadn't said good-bye to Emily, just let his feet lead him down the hall away from her.

Despite all the evidence to the contrary, he was pretty law-abiding most of the time, and while the idea of just walking out of the building did fleetingly cross his mind, he knew it would only prolong the agony.

He wended his way through the pool of administrative staff desks. His mother wasn't at hers. But Maria, who handled attendance, gave him a doleful smile. She knew what was happening and seemed to feel sorry for him, which only made it worse.

He knocked on the director's door. "Come in," Powell said.

His mother was already there, but she didn't even look up when he entered, just stared at her hands.

"Come here, Jeremy," Powell said in her firm way. He stood in front of the desk, next to his mother. It didn't seem right to sit.

"Well," Powell said with a frown. "What do you have to say for yourself?"

She held out one of the posters from that morning, which had been lying on her desk. He suppressed a wince at the sight of that horrible picture.

"Um." It wasn't really the brightest thing to say, but what else could he do? Deny putting up the posters? Even if he hadn't been the person to do this one, there were plenty of other pranks he was responsible for. And nobody would believe it was Emily.

"I saw these this morning," Powell continued. "But I waited to have this conversation until after the assembly, because I know you had a lead role in the film and I didn't want to ruin the experience for you and all your friends. I'm not completely heartless," she said, and smiled. Her smile was even more terrifying than her frown.

"The posters themselves are not the biggest problem; I hope you realize that. They're inappropriate, but that's only part of it. It's the name. The Merry Pranksters. A band of kids who play pranks. My own words. I'm not stupid, Jeremy, and I feel very strongly this is an admission of guilt, that you're flaunting your bad behavior in our faces. And I have to say, I don't like it."

"But—" he began. She held up a hand.

"I'm sorry, Karen," she said to his mother. "I know this is hard on you, too. But when we stopped allowing boys to matriculate at St. Edith's, many of the trustees thought we should ask all of them to leave. And I fought that. I thought it was unfair to the boys who were part of our community. But I'm beginning to think maybe I was wrong."

Jeremy stood and let the words wash over him.

"Your friends are going to be in trouble too, don't you worry about that. This has gone too far, and there will be repercussions. Suspensions, at the very least," Powell said. "But you're a particular case, and I'm sorry to say I don't think—"

*BANG!*

The door to Powell's office burst open and slammed against a wooden bookcase. Even Jeremy's mother looked up at the intrusion.

"It was me," Claudia said, standing in the doorway. "It wasn't Jeremy; it was me."

"Miss Hoffmann, you're interrupting a very important—"

"I know I am, but what I have to say is even more important," she said, striding into the room. "Jeremy didn't have anything to do with the pranks. They were all my idea. I wanted to shake things up here, you know? Make St. Edith's less . . ."

"That's very kind of you, Claudia, to try and take the blame, but I'm afraid I'm not that easy to fool." Ms. Powell got a strange smile on her face. "Even I can see Jeremy is front and center on this poster."

"Of course, because I thought it was funny," Claudia said quickly. "I used the pictures from the Film Club program. I thought it might be a teaser for our next project."

"Hmmm," Powell said. She didn't seem to be buying it.

"Jeremy couldn't have done any of this stuff," she said. "He lives in Lower Falls. I'm the one who lives down the street from school. Besides, he's never been in trouble before. Do you think he's going to start now, when he's the only boy in the whole entire school? Plus, he's not the one who's in here every other week; I am."

It was true. Claudia was always getting called in to see the director about violating the dress code or talking in class. But she'd never been in serious trouble.

Claudia was working up a full head of steam. "Do you have any evidence he pulled any of those other pranks? Or are you just accusing him because he's a boy? That's kind of sexist, isn't it? To just assume it was the one boy, to never consider it could be a girl?"

"Claudia . . . ," Powell said. But Jeremy saw a tiny glimmer of something in her eyes. Something like wavering.

"You're the one who said other schools play pranks," Claudia said. "Maybe I wanted St. Edith's to be more like them."

"I did say that. But I was talking about an organized event, not something kids do on their own. A girl became very sick when those doorknobs were changed. That's serious business. And the lobby . . ."

"I'm sorry about that; I really am," Claudia said. "But if you need to expel anyone, it should be me. Here," she said, and handed Powell a DVD. "Footage. I filmed myself doing the pranks. It's all there. The gnomes, the snow. Everything. And it's all me."

Jeremy gaped at her. So did his mother, who had an expression on her face he couldn't quite read. He knew just how Claudia would have edited the film to make it seem like she was the only one behind the pranks. Her movie, once again.

Powell let out a deep breath and pursed her lips. She seemed to be thinking.

Nobody said a word, they all held perfectly still, so still Jeremy could hear the ticking of the heavy clock on the mantel over the fireplace.

Powell exhaled again and straightened in her chair. "I hope you realize you're in very big trouble, Miss Hoffmann. But I have to admit it's somewhat of a different situation, if you're the one responsible. I saw those posters, and I just assumed that it was Jeremy. I really never wanted to take such drastic measures, but considering the situation, it just seemed the only option. . . ." She trailed off, then looked at Jeremy and at his mother. "I think I need to speak to Claudia privately, if you don't mind."

Jeremy and his mother didn't wait for her to ask twice.

When they reached his mother's desk, she sat down and he stood awkwardly next to her. He didn't know what else to do.

"That's a very good friend you have, Jeremy," his

mother said softly, looking at her computer. "Don't ever forget it."

"Mom, I . . ."

"I hope you've learned your lesson, at any rate," she said briskly. "We'll talk more about this at home. Even if Powell doesn't punish you, that doesn't mean you'll get off scot-free. Maybe you weren't totally responsible for the pranks, but I'm pretty sure you've been up to something. Powell may be swayed by Claudia Hoffmann, but I know you better than she does."

He nodded.

"Do you want to wait for a ride, or do you want to take your bike?"

What he wanted was to wait for Claudia, but he somehow innately knew that wasn't an option.

"Bike," he said. He hoped whatever happened, Claudia would know where to find him.

# TWENTY-EIGHT

**JEREMY WALKED SLOWLY THROUGH THE BUILDING** and out to the bike rack. He figured that if he rode to Mickey's, Claudia would join him after her meeting with Powell. He hoped her ploy had worked and whatever trouble she was in, she wouldn't actually get kicked out. Even when they were having their worst fights, he couldn't imagine St. Edith's without her.

But standing just outside the school was Anna.

"Hi," she said. She sounded different than she had that morning. He stood dumbly, waiting for the storm of her words to hit him again. But it didn't.

"Emily told me that she was the one who made the posters," she said. "I guess I should have known. You wouldn't have put a picture of yourself like that all over the place. You looked pretty stupid."

"Yeah." He didn't know where he stood with Emily, but he knew it would have taken a lot for her to go to Anna and confess.

"And I know nobody really thought it was me in that

bikini. It doesn't even look like me!" She laughed—a small laugh, but still a laugh. "I'm sorry I got so mad, it's just . . . I left all my friends back in Connecticut when my mom got married. When you're new, you always think everybody's laughing at you behind your back."

Jeremy considered this. He'd never been the new kid. Maybe some things were tougher than being the only boy.

And looking at her now, he realized she wasn't whatever he had built her up to be in his head, like some kind of mythological creature he had to impress, or be afraid of. She was just another girl, another St. Edith's girl, and if he was going to be the only boy at school, he was going to have to stop being afraid of her. He'd done so many things this fall he never thought he would have done in a million years. Risky things. And sure, maybe not all of them were good ideas. Actually, maybe none of them were. But they showed he was more capable than he had realized.

So he made a decision.

"There's this place, Mickey's?" he said. "It's right outside town. Some of us go after school to hang out. Maybe you'd like to come sometime?"

"Really?" She sounded surprised, but not in a bad way.

"I'd have to check with my mom, but um, sure. That would be cool."

"Great." He felt more pleased with himself than he had in ages. After all, not all risk taking had to get you expelled. "See you tomorrow," he added as he walked over to his bike.

Jeremy rode as slowly as possible to Mickey's, knowing it would take time for Claudia to finish her meeting with Powell. The restaurant was deserted, as usual, except for Whitey—Dylan—who was standing at the counter when Jeremy walked in, looking at a magazine.

"Hey," Jeremy said.

"Oh, hi," Whitey replied.

Quasimodo was in a foul mood and smelled like Jeremy's dad the summer he gave up deodorant. Jeremy dropped his money on the counter, took his chips and soda, and retreated to a table on the other side of the café. Whitey joined him.

"So, fill me in. Where's Claudia? Are you guys still fighting?"

"It's a long story," Jeremy said. "She might end up getting expelled for the pranks we did."

"Oh wow, really?" Whitey said. "She's so cool. All the girls at my school are so . . . I dunno. You're lucky."

Jeremy laughed. "You must have me confused with somebody else."

"No, really," Whitey said. "You go to a good school for free and you have these smart friends who like to make movies and plan crazy pranks. All the guys at my school do is hang around in the parking lot behind the Stop and Shop."

"I bet you could help with the movies if you wanted," Jeremy offered. "Claudia's always looking for boys."

"Really? You think so?" Whitey asked. "That would be great. My mom's old boyfriend used to have a video camera, and my sister and I would make all these little movies—stupid stuff, but it was fun."

"Yeah," Jeremy said. They sat in silence for a while. He didn't know how to explain it, but he felt that if he sat super still and focused all of his energy, he could will Powell to not expel Claudia, and he could fix everything that had gone wrong.

And then, almost as if his wish had come true, Claudia walked through the door smiling.

"Hey," she greeted both of them.

Jeremy stared at her. "Well?"

"Well, what?" she said, still grinning. She cocked her head at him like she was confused. The she plopped down in a chair and started taking chips out of his bag without asking. "You look like you're waiting for me to tell you something?"

"Of course I'm waiting for you to tell me something!" She was infuriating. But it was Claudia, and he knew she would insist on telling the story in her own time. He gave her a fake glare, but she just smiled at him and kept eating his chips.

"I know you didn't make the posters," he finally said. "I'm sorry I blamed you. I know you would never do something like that."

"Yeah, but what you don't know is that I laughed when I saw them. I thought you deserved it," she said.

He raised his eyebrows, but all he said was, "I can't believe you burst into Powell's office without knocking. She was ten seconds away from kicking me out for good."

"Well, maybe I don't want you to leave! Haven't you figured that out by now?"

"Then why did we do all those pranks in the first place?"

She laughed. "Because they were fun, maybe? Because it was something we could do together? I never thought you'd really go through with it. Taking the blame, getting kicked out. And I guess playing the pranks made me feel like the way things were . . . before. I liked the way things were."

"Before what?"

She scratched at the table. "Before you started caring about you being a boy and other people being girls. Before it started to be all those categories."

"Claudia—"

But she shook her head. "I know it's inevitable. I know we're going to be teenagers and that's the way things work. But I still need you as my best friend. I need your perspective on things. I need you to be my partner in crime—"

"Literally," he reminded her.

"Well, it's not going to be literally anymore," she said. "Because you're not going to get expelled, and neither am I."

"For real?" He breathed a long sigh of relief. He'd suspected she'd manage to pull it off—it was Claudia, after all—but hearing her say it made all the difference.

"So," he said, leaning back in his chair. "What happens next?"

Claudia laughed that old conspiratorial laugh of hers. "That's the best part. Powell couldn't expel me—not with the money my dad gives. I don't think she wanted to expel anybody, honestly, but maybe she felt like she had to do something if it was you? None of it was what she expected, and so she didn't really have a plan. They're always the easiest to manipulate when they don't have a plan."

"But you're going to be punished, aren't you? I'm probably going to be grounded for the rest of my life once my mom gets home."

"Yeah, I'm going to be punished. Suspended for a week, and detention forever. But I don't care."

And she didn't seem to. In fact, she seemed almost jubilant.

"Oh, and I have to do some school version of community service next semester. Like weed the flower beds? A total waste, but I figure you owe me big-time, so you can help out. Maybe we can even make a movie about it. Something set in a prison? If I can find some orange jumpsuits."

"Okay, okay," he said. Leave it to Claudia to turn

detention into a movie-making opportunity. "But you're crazy! You could have really been expelled."

"I know; it was a bold move," Claudia said. "But Powell told me applications for next year are already up fifty percent thanks to the pranks. Believe it or not, we've managed to actually help St. Edith's reputation. And save Powell's job. Which, in the end, may be more important than getting anyone expelled."

Jeremy shook his head. "I don't believe it. Sometimes I think you might be the luckiest person on earth, Claudia."

"Me? I think you're the lucky one," she said. "Maybe only because of me, though. Oh, but there's another thing. We have to help her institute a regular Prank Day for everybody," she added, making a face. "Like an annual school ritual. So she's totally co-opting it, of course, like the suit she is. Absolutely typical."

Jeremy made a face back at her, but he couldn't find much to be upset about. Prank Day might even be fun. Maybe he'd come up with something especially cool to do, since he was the only boy at St. Edith's.

For the first time in ages, that didn't bother him one bit.

# PREP CONFIDENTIAL

**RED MILL, MA:** St. Edith's, the school your great-grandmother probably thought was too boring to go to back in 1901, has a fresh new reputation—and a surge in enrollment—thanks to a series of unique and well-executed pranks performed by some surprisingly inventive souls among the bland-as-oatmeal student body.

The Merry Pranksters—identities still, as of yet, unknown—witnessed a setback last month when a prank gone awry sent a student to the hospital. Still, many on campus hope this glitch won't keep the tricksters from more hijinks.

"My friends at other schools used to mock me for going to St. Dither's," said one anonymous student, using a popular negative nickname for the dour academy of higher learning. "Now they all want to know what I'm going to do for Prank Day."

An anonymous student at a nearby school said, with no sarcasm in her voice whatsoever, "I wish our school was more like St Edith's."

Director Amanda Powell insisted the enrollment

increase was not entirely due to the pranks. "We added several new programs this year and refurbished our soccer field."

Still, she admitted, "It's nice students think St. Edith's is a fun place to attend school."

(Well, we at the *Con* wouldn't go that far; not just yet.)

# ACKNOWLEDGMENTS

THIS BOOK HAS MANY "PROUD AUNTS AND uncles," in the lovely words of my friend Minda, but there are a few who deserve special mention:

Seeing this book through the eyes of my editor at Aladdin, Amy Cloud, has been a fantastic experience, especially since she has the uncanny ability to make many of her wonderful suggestions sound like they were actually my idea. I also want to thank the rest of the Aladdin team, especially Laura Lyn DiSiena, the designer, and Katherine Devendorf, the managing editor, as well as the illustrator, Paul Hoppe, who captured the spirit of Jeremy and St. Edith's so well in his cover drawing.

I also need to thank Crissy Adams, who is living proof that when one of your friends confides in you that she wrote a book and asks if you would like to read it, only the best (or the craziest) person would say, "Sure, why not?"

Minda Martin Zwerin, self-proclaimed "proud aunty" of this book and winner of the Most Likely to Talk Me Off a Writing Ledge Award.

## ACKNOWLEDGMENTS

Gregory Katsoulis, that one critique partner every writer needs who won't ever give you a pass on anything. Bonus points if he's also a professional photographer who does head shots and a neighbor who likes to have people over for dinner.

Brenda St. John Brown, because it's hard to believe I met one of my most dedicated critique partners thanks to a writing blog that didn't belong to either of us. It's even more amazing we've shared our writing successes and failures for so many years despite the ocean between us.

My agent, the unflappable Bridget Smith, who dots every *i* and crosses every *t* and still manages to do six impossible things before breakfast.

My parents, Don and Judy Gjertsen, and my sister, Dina Gjertsen, for their constant support of me as both a writer and as a person.

And most of all I want to thank my awesome husband, Scott Malone, and our daughter, Nora. They make everything I do worth it.